DUEL WITH COLOSSUS

THE GOLDEN AMAZON SAGA

DUEL WITH COLOSSUS

THE GOLDEN AMAZON SAGA, BOOK SEVENTEEN

JOHN RUSSELL FEARN

Edited by Philip Harbottle

THE BORGO PRESS
MMXIV

DUEL WITH COLOSSUS

CONTENTS

THE GOLDEN AMAZON

by Philip Harbottle

In 1943 British writer John Russell Fearn decided to quit writing for the American pulp science fiction magazines, and to concentrate instead on books for the English market. Within a very few years he became established as a leading novelist in several genres, not only science fiction, but also mystery and detective fiction, and westerns.

His first new SF novel, *The Golden Amazon*, was published by World's Work in April 1944. In this story, a little girl of three years of age is made the subject of an idealistic scientist's illegal glandular experiments. The scientist's dream is to end world wars by creating a woman devoid of the usual lusts and frailties of mankind, who upon reaching maturity would institute a benign scientific rule. But the apparently successful experiment has a flaw: it instills into the girl a hatred for all men, and a ruthless cruelty. Her supernatural scientific gifts enable her to master atomic power, and practically leads her to destroy the world. She breaks the will and strength of men, and elevates women to positions of wealth and power. She also discovers human synthesis, and by this means she is able to escape retribution when she is eventually overthrown. She is seen to collapse and die, a victim of consuming ketabolism, echoing the memorable finale of Rider Haggard's *She*. In actuality, it was only her synthetic image, and this paved the way for the *Golden Amazon Returns*, and further sequels.

Fearn sold reprint rights in the first novel to the prestigious Canadian magazine, the Toronto *Star Weekly*. The magazine carried a special Comics Supplement, the centre section of which was a "complete novel," published in newspaper format. Aimed at a general readership, the novels were written by the top popular novelists of the day, including John Dickson Carr, Ellery Queen, and P. G. Wodehouse. They sold hundreds of thousands of copies, and the novels were syndicated to several American newspapers in the Maine and New York areas. The Amazon novels enjoyed extraordinary popularity (especially with Canadian housewives), and ran for the next sixteen years following the appearance of the first novel in the March 3, 1945 issue, ending with Fearn's sudden death in September 1960, aged only fifty-two. His final two Amazon novels appeared posthumously.

During Fearn's lifetime, only the first six novels were published in British hardcover editions from the World's Work in England, after appearing in the *Star Weekly*. This was because the publishers discontinued their entire fiction line in 1954. However, the Amazon novels continued to appear in the *Star Weekly*, eventually notching up twenty-four titles.

Fearn had resold paperback rights to the Canadian publisher Harlequin Books, but after publishing only the first three titles, they stopped publishing SF and other genre fiction to concentrate on their famous Romances line.

Meanwhile, as early as 1949, Fearn had realized that the Amazon series had the potential to run indefinitely. This presented him with a problem, however. The "origin story" of the Golden Amazon was conceived and actually set during the Second World War. Subsequent novels were written during the war and the immediate postwar period, and projected their stories only a few decades into the future.

He very astutely realized that to keep ahead of reality, he needed to move the Amazon *further* into the future—first into the outer solar system, and thence to the stars. So with the seventh novel, he introduced a new main character, Abna of Atlantis—someone equally intelligent, and even stronger than herself. These dynamics provided him with an *interstellar* canvas, thus ensuring that the series would remain ahead of reality.

Fearn's strategy was a great success, and the Amazon novels retained their popularity, ending only with his tragically early death in 1960. By then he had written a further twenty Amazon novels and made preliminary notes for his next (which would later be written by Fearn's biographer, Philip Harbottle).

Long after Fearn's death, his entire Amazon series would eventually see print from the pioneering US small press Gryphon Books in limited paperback editions, and later by the Canadian Battered Silicon Dispatch Box small press in their hardcover Omnibus series.

This new Borgo Press paperback series will be the first trade edition of all twenty-one of these later novels by Fearn, beginning with the seventh novel in the original series. First published in 1949 as *Conquest of the Amazon*, I have edited it slightly as *World Beneath Ice* (The Golden Amazon Saga, Book One) so that it can be read and enjoyed by new readers who may be totally unfamiliar with what had gone before. Subsequent novels have also been slightly edited for modern readers.

The publishers hope that this new series may create many more "fans of the Amazon." Meanwhile, any reader interested in seeking out the earlier six Golden Amazon novels will find that they are readily available on the internet, and in numerous earlier paperback and hardcover editions.

* * * *

To date, readers can enjoy the following new Borgo Press editions:

Book One: *World Beneath Ice*

In destroying the threat of an alien invasion, the Golden Amazon had inadvertently caused a decline in the sun's heat, encasing Earth in an ice sheet that threatens to eliminate humanity. The Amazon encounters Abna, a descendant of Atlantis, stronger and even more scientifically advanced than she, and the ruler of an Atlantean colony still surviving in a protected environment on Jupiter. She refuses his offer of marriage, but agrees to form an alliance in order to restore the sun and save the Earth. One thing that Abna has not told the Amazon is that all the females of his race have been wiped out by a bacilli infection....

Book Two: *Lord of Atlantis*

A gigantic ridge of land rises from the Atlantic floor, causing massive tidal waves on either side of the ocean. Even stranger, both England and America are then assailed by an invasion of prehistoric monsters! A gigantic domed city rests on the newly risen plateau, whilst out in space an alien spacecraft orbits the Earth. Such are the mysteries and challenges facing the Golden Amazon, self-appointed governess of Earth, as she struggles to unravel the maze of mystery that was the deadly legacy of Atlantis!

Book Three: *Triangle of Power*

The marriage of Violet Ray Brant—better known as The Golden Amazon—and Abna of Atlantis should have ushered in an era of peace and scientific prosperity to the people of Earth. But an unexpected turn of events finds Abna betrayed and marooned on a satellite of Jupiter, and the Amazon flung far beyond the Solar System. With Earth's two protectors removed, the planet is now at the mercy of another Atlantean, the master scientist Sefner Quorne....

Book Four: *The Amethyst City*

The metaphysical union of the Amazon and Abna results in the mental creation of a fully mature daughter— Viona. Quorne, still struggling for domination, forces Viona into a marriage ceremony, and impregnates her. But with the intervention of Tarnec Brodix, a super-mind from an external universe, Quorne and Viona are separately flung into an ultra-dimensional limbo. Abna chooses to follow after his daughter, leaving the Amazon to brood over the disaster, alone in the Amethyst City of Saturn.

Book Five: *Daughter of the Amazon*

A miscalculation by the super-mathematician Tarnec Brodix destroys his universe, and the fault spreads into the Earth universe in the form of a Dark Tide of Absolute Nothingness. Unable to save himself, Brodix transfers his knowledge into the one mind powerful enough to receive it: that if Sefian, the son who has been born to Viona and Quorne. Sefian rapidly evolves, and, no longer human, after saving the Earth universe, vanishes into the greater universe, to seek new challenges. Then the Amazon is confronted with a further puzzle—a large section of the planet Neptune is discovered to be an exact duplicate of the Earth!

Book Six: *Quorne Returns*

The bacterial intelligences of Neptune plan to conquer Earth by replacing humans in key positions with alien duplicates. The Neptunians are themselves subjugated by the sinister Atlantean scientist, Sefner Quorne. Alerted to the threat, the Golden Amazon hits back by creating the ultimate doomsday weapon—only to precipitate a reprisal from the denizens of another universe....

Book Seven: *The Central Intelligence*

The Golden Amazon's arch-enemy, Sefner Quorne, discovers that all mental gifts, such as memory and creativity, are something that is broadcast throughout the universe by a Central Intelligence—and then interpreted according to the quality of the individual brain of the recipient. At the surprising suggestion of his wife, Viona, the Amazon's daughter, Quorne travels with her to the very center of the universe, in order to wrest the secrets of mentality from the very source itself!

Book Eight: *The Cosmic Crusaders*

The Golden Amazon renounces all ties with Earth when, together with her husband, Abna, and her daughter, Viona, she sets off on a journey to explore the cosmos. On the strange worlds of Alpha Centauri, she encounters Mizanu, the embodiment of evil—a planet-sized hypertrophied brain! Its baleful, crushing mental power threatens to reach out beyond the double-system of Alpha and Proxima Centauri to engulf the Earth and all the other inhabited planets of the galaxy—unless the Amazon can destroy it first!

Book Nine: *Parasite Planet*

The Cosmic Crusaders discover a fantastic world of mental parasites drawing form and substance from our own Earth, fifty light years distant. The planet is ruled by a being identical to the Golden Amazon herself—but an Amazon who's coldly scientific and vicious, mirroring the original Amazon as she had once been early in her career. Inevitably, they become locked in a deadly duel—to the death!

Book Ten: *World Out of Step*

The Cosmic Crusaders find themselves on a planet that seems mysteriously not to conform with natural law, a world out of step with the universe. It leaps ahead into time at unexpected moments, thereby suddenly adding many years of age to the flower-like inhabitants, and killing tens of thousands of individuals through death and old age. In trying to find the alien menace responsible, The Golden Amazon and her fellow Crusaders are flung backwards and forwards through time and space, threatening their own survival....

Book Eleven: *The Shadow People*

The Cosmic Crusaders discover a planet whose people are subject to a baleful influence from outer space that sweeps across their world—and for a brief while embraces every man, woman and child. It stirs the emotions of the sexes against each other. Men desire only to destroy women, and women men. Only those with higher types of mind are able to build a resistance against it. The struggle is dire and dreadful, and leaves its victims physical and mental wrecks. The less fortunate are left dead after the Wave has passed.

But when the Crusaders identify and destroy the source of the problem, they precipitate an even greater menace....

Book Twelve: *Kingpin Planet*

The Cosmic Crusaders are plunged into a strange new space, where all the probabilities of electronic law were strangely altered, a complete and stunning inversion of the so-called natural laws. They discover the mysterious silver planet of Tuca, and deep below its surface they find an enigmatic machine—the legacy of a vanished race. Masters of science, they had overreached themselves by constructing a strange machine that could alter the very laws of nature and electronic probability. The machine had ultimately destroyed them, and blasted a neighboring planet into a cosmic cinder—and unless the Cosmic Crusaders can stop it, it may well destroy the entire universe!

Book Thirteen: *World in Reverse*

Continuing their cosmic crusade amongst the stars, the Golden Amazon and her companions discover a planet in another space where living beings are being synthetically created. The mystery deepens with the discovery that the synthetic race is evolving backwards! Determined to solve these mysteries, the Crusaders find themselves up against the Mithons, a sadistic alien race led by a being known as the Supreme One. Can the Amazon save the day?

Book Fourteen: *Dwellers in Darkness*

Voyaging into a sector of interstellar space plunged into total darkness, the Cosmic Crusaders encounter a powerful and sinister mastermind, who is regarded as a God by the race he has forced to evolve without eyes. And not content with shaping the evolution of their bodies, the mastermind has also impressed on their minds an urge to conquer and dominate...

Book Fifteen: *World in Duplicate*

In the depths of the Milky Way, the Cosmic Crusaders discover yet another mysterious planet—this time a world that appears to be a duplicate of Earth, birthplace of the Golden Amazon! Their investigations uncover a sinister plot by an alien race that threaten the Amazon's home world with complete annihilation!

Book Sixteen: *Lords of Creation*

At first, it appeared to be a sun, forming in space where none had existed before. It kindled as an atomic fire, sustaining itself by the breakdown of fusion energies. Then, even as the Cosmic Crusaders watched, the newly-created sun was no longer just a ball of fire: it was gyrating, like a stupendous Catherine Wheel, a flaming mss spewing filaments from its edges. Then they realized the amazing truth: they were witnessing the creation of planets, flaming streamers of incandescent matter that would condense into worlds! The Golden Amazon and her fellow Crusaders grapple with the very forces of creation in their most astounding adventure to date!

CHAPTER 1

THE COLOSSAL SPACESHIP

The golden-haired woman in the black tights with the broad, jeweled instrument belt about her slender waist, sat peering intently into the eyepiece of the high-power telescope. Around her grouped three others— her husband Abna of Jupiter, Viona her daughter, and Mexone, husband of Viona. In a word, including the ever-young, superbly beautiful woman at the telescope, the Cosmic Crusaders, with the Golden Amazon at their head.

There was not a sound in the vast control room of the spaceship Ultra, that spaceship of impregnable hardness and fantastic speed, cruising now in the remote deeps of the Milky Way. The Crusaders had just ended one adventure, which had concluded with the death of Und, last of an alien race, but ahead of them lay yet another mystery if they cared to investigate it— and naturally they did care. Since their chief object in life was to bring the blessings of incredible scientific achievement to those races who, for some reason or other, were not so fortunate as themselves, mystery or the unexplained had a complete fascination for them... as now.

Ahead of the Ultra, at a tremendous distance it seemed, loomed a curious triangular formation, a triangle traced out by three points of varicolored light. The top point was emerald and the left and right points were blue and yellow... And curiously enough they had come into being with complete suddenness where formerly there had only been the abysmal blackness of space.

At last the Amazon spoke, raising her unfathomable eyes from the telescopic eyepiece.

"I may wrong," she confessed quietly. "I said earlier that those three points might be planets, but now I think I'm mistaken. They have the hard edges common to a planet's disk, but nothing more. The surfaces don't reveal any planetary characteristics. Quite frankly, I don't know what they are."

"Could the analyzers tell us?" Viona asked, thinking.

"They might. We can but see."

Viona crossed to the huge instrument panel and switched on the automatic analyzers—instruments, which, embodying telescopic principles, used the magic of electronics to "read" the composition of the object required. Carefully, Viona tuned the instruments and then stood back to watch the ground glass screen. Behind her, the Amazon, Abna, and Mexone stood waiting too... And the results were rather surprising. On the screen, the elements converted into words by a transformer, appeared a list of metals, some known and others unknown. As far as the various colors were concerned, they simply registered in their wavelengths of green, blue, and yellow.

"Well, this is certainly a puzzle," the Amazon said, frowning. "They're not planets; they're not suns. The reading shows only a mass of metals, which possibly comprise all one element, just as adulterated steel might appear as that metal and yet actually be composed of a good many isotopes."

"Notice something else?" Abna asked. "Look at that mass reading. If we were dealing with planets or stars the mass reading would be in the quintillions of tons; but it only reads in tens of thousands, which as far as cosmic masses are concerned, isn't particularly big."

There was silence for a moment. It was not often the Crusaders came up against something they couldn't understand, but it had certainly happened now—and all the time the Ultra was drifting nearer to the enigma, not under its own power, but carried by the subtle currents of radiation forever prevalent in space.

"And the three points came into being abruptly, in the twinkling of an eye," the Amazon mused. "How? That's another problem which we—"

She jerked her head round abruptly, half surprised, as the red warning light on the switchboard suddenly winked—and kept on winking. Amazed, she looked at the others.

"What's causing that?" she demanded. "It only winks when we're in danger of colliding with something—yet we're in empty space, with those planets, or whatever they are, countless millions of miles away—"

"No we're not!" Viona interrupted suddenly, staring through the huge window. "We're nearly on top of something—I can see it now, a shade lighter than the dark of space—great heavens—!"

Complete awe was in her voice as she angled her face upwards. "It's a spaceship! The most colossal one I've ever seen—"

The Amazon swung and hurtled to the window, staring with Viona out into the deeps. Mexone and Abna moved up too and surveyed the scene.

"Now I get it!" the Amazon exclaimed. "Those triangular light points are outlook ports in a spaceship—not stars! No wonder they didn't give a reading— That explains the mass-figure. We got the reading of a spaceship mass truly gigantic in every sense of the word. Yes, we're nearly into it—"

She twirled suddenly and dove for the switchboard. The Ultra's power plant came suddenly into life, swinging aside the nose of the vessel and turning it parallel to the fantastically big vessel drifting in the deeps. With only a matter of minutes to spare a head-on collision was averted.

"Good work, Vi," Abna said, staring through the window. "But never in my life did I see a space machine as big as this. You could put the Ultra inside one of its rivets and still have room to spare… Anyway, the mystery of the lights is explained. They're shining through three windows in this vast hull, each window giving a different light."

The danger averted for the moment the Amazon went back to the window. In silence the four of them watched as mile after mile of vast metallic hull slid by, and there was still no sign of this incredibly big spaceship coming to an end. The triangular setting of lights had vanished now since, of course, the Ultra was parallel to them.

"Well, what do we do?" the Amazon questioned at last, as the length of the ship still showed no signs of ending. "A thing this big which appears suddenly from nowhere in the Milky Way is well worth investigating—but where do we start?"

"Might cruise around a bit and try and have a look through one of the large portholes," Mexone suggested.

"Good idea."

As the monster spaceship still showed no signs of ending, the Amazon moved over to the switchboard and operated the controls. Immediately the Ultra ceased its forward progress and instead turned outwards into space, away from the giant spaceship... The Amazon kept the Ultra slowly on the move until there was a change in the perspective and the whole looming mass of the cosmic giant could be clearly seen outlined against the distant stars, its portholes in triangular formation blazing brightly.

"Easy to see how we were misled," Abna admitted a trifle ruefully. "At a distance you can't see the thing against the black of space and just behind it there aren't many stars to form a background... By heaven, but it's a size!"

The Amazon did not comment. She started the Ultra moving forward again, a gnat compared to a mastodon, and presently one of the monster's portholes was dead in line—the emerald one—which increased to a circle of green and sickly brilliance as the Ultra floated nearer.

"I'll stop here," the Amazon said, snapping switches. "It's about as near as we can get… Now, let's see what there is."

She swung the telescope towards the outlook window and focused it on the vast green "star" ahead. Through the telescope, details leapt into sharp relief. The Amazon realized she was gazing into a machine room of indescribable perplexity, all of it lit with that bilious light. Yet somehow it was not hurtful to the eye, and it picked out details with amazing clarity. The Amazon made no effort to analyze the machinery at her distance: in fact she was fascinated by something else—the size of the men at work on the machines. All things in proportion they must have been enormous. The only other point was that, big or otherwise, they had understandable physique, being shaped exactly like Earthlings, but of course on a vastly larger scale.

"Well?" came the voice of Abna. "What goes on?"

"Men and machines," the Amazon responded, looking up, "See for yourselves—each one of you."

She relinquished the telescope and stood waiting as Abna, Viona and Mexone gazed through the lens in turn. Finally they looked at each other, faint bafflement on their faces.

"Well, they're an intelligent race all right," Abna commented.

"Pretty huge too as far as can be judged. But we haven't the least idea what they're driving at or how they appeared so suddenly from wherever they came from."

Viona said: "It's possible, of course, that they came into this area of space without any lights on—then suddenly they switched their different colored lights on from inside, and there they were. Anyway, it's how it would look to us."

"Granted," the Amazon said, musing. "Anyway, we're not going to get very far acting like a bunch of cosmic Peeping Toms and looking through windows. We ought to contact these people."

"Why?" Mexone asked. "After all, it's no business of ours what they're up to, and they haven't shown any hostility."

"True, but an exchange of scientific information might prove useful," the Amazon responded. "They're obviously here for a vital reason, and with a ship this size it ought to be an *interesting* reason." Suddenly she made up her mind. "We'll try radio contact and see if anything happens."

As she crossed over to the instruments Abna made a comment.

"It surprises me that they haven't done something about us before now: they could easily with a vessel their size, and they must certainly know we're here buzzing around them—"

He had hardly spoken the words before something happened. Suddenly, without any warning, the Ultra lurched violently.

The impact flung the Amazon away from the radio equipment and sent Abna stumbling across the floor. Viona and Mexone came up sharp against the control board chairs and so saved themselves. In those same seconds the Ultra started moving, drawn by some immense force or other towards the nearby spaceship.

"We're not going because they decide it, anyway," the Amazon snapped, lurching over to the control board. "We'll only go when we decide it ourselves—They're not going to get away with this."

As the others watched her she slammed over the switches on the power-plant control panel, building up reverse speed as rapidly as she dared. Normally, considering the immense reserves of the atomic plant, the Ultra should have drawn steadily away from the monster spaceship, even as in the past she had drawn away from the attraction of dangerous worlds by completely negating the gravity thereof… But this time no such thing happened. The Ultra continued to move towards the spaceship with a slow but relentless speed.

"Magnetism obviously," Abna said, crossing to the Amazon's side as she increased the resources of the power plant still further. "They've got magnetism at work which is stronger than our power plant—"

The Amazon and Abna were silent for a moment, listening to the helpless screaming of the Ultra's power plant as it raged to no purpose. In the ordinary way, considering the power it was exerting, the Ultra by now would have achieved nearly the speed of light—yet it was held in thrall, utterly helpless.

"Cut the power," Abna said grimly. "You'll wreck the bearings racing it at that rate to no purpose."

Grim-faced, the Amazon disengaged the switches and the din from the power plant whined down into silence. Then she looked with Abna through the observation window. The stars and void had become blotted out by a vast wall of metal—the super spaceship's hull. Finally there was a gentle bump and the Ultra ceased to move, glued to the big ship with the tenacity of a barnacle.

"Well, we wanted to meet the unknowns, and it looks as though we're going to," Abna sighed.

"Yes, but I prefer meeting unknowns on our own terms," the Amazon retorted. "This is compulsion in the highest sense… We'd better be prepared for anything. Viona, Mexone—are you fully armed?"

"Completely," they responded together.

"Then in that case—" The Amazon stopped abruptly and blinked, sheer amazement on her face. There was good reason for it, too, as her violet eyes fixed on an object like a small steel ball sailing gently into the big control room.

"What the—" Abna started to say; then he yanked a protonic gun from his belt and waited warily. The Amazon did likewise and gave him a glance.

"It may be dangerous, it may not," she muttered.

"Somehow, it came through the solid wall of the Ultra—and we've always thought of the Ultra as impenetrable by any known force."

"But not proof against dimensional tricks," Abna told her, watching the slowly moving ball intently. "That was probably how it was done—fourth dimensional projection."

"But what is it?" Viona demanded. "It looks like a tennis ball made of steel—"

She stopped talking from sheer amazement as, suddenly, the steel ball uttered sounds—weird, dragging sounds just like a voice speaking on a phonograph record that was running down.

"…rin…you…grrrr…ings," said the ball, and then there was silence for a moment.

"It's radio anyway," the Amazon said at length, frowning. "But what we're supposed to understand from that I don't know. It sounds like Chinese spoken backwards."

"Suppose we allow for certain scientific facts," Viona suggested, watching the ball with fascinated interest. "If these people are as big as we think they are their voices will be long, deep, and slow compared to normal speech—or what we regard as normal speed. Allow for that, and we might make something of the words…"

The Amazon glanced at Abna rather wryly. "She's right, you, know, and teaching us our business for a change! Wait! It's off again…"

The ball spoke once more, but this time the voice

was at normal speed—a pleasant, well-rounded voice, with a remarkably clear diction.

"We bring you greetings… We trust that this speed is more normal to you. We have altered its rate to suit your purpose. If you understand us now, say so. The ball is a radio television transmitter and receiver combined, with which we can hear and see you as well as transmit our own voices though not our images. Speak. We are listening."

"Yes, we can understand you now," the Amazon replied quietly. "We had thought of seeking an audience with you, but now it seems that we have little choice about the matter. I would remark that we do not take kindly to your methods of persuasion."

"We humbly regret any inconvenience. However, it seems absurd to try and communicate in this fashion when we can be much more comfortable and intimate. We have no wish to harm you, and certainly we would like to speak with you, face to face… Are you prepared to entrust yourselves to our science and come aboard?"

The Amazon hesitated, so Abna answered for her.

"We are prepared. If it comes to that, we haven't much choice."

"Simply walk towards the wall of your vessel through which the radio-television ball appeared—or more accurately the wall which is pressed against our vessel's hull."

"And when we reach the wall what happens?" the Amazon asked bluntly.

"You will see. Just keep walking."

There was nothing else for it. The quartet looked at each other, gave a final check over the weapons in their belts, and then strolled in a line towards the wall of the control room.

They had almost reached it when it misted strangely, impregnable though it was supposed to be, and there shone through it—as though through a fog—a deep green radiance. Interested, prepared for anything, they kept on walking...

And suddenly the fog was gone though the green light remained.

They had passed through the walls of both the Ultra and the big spaceship without any hindrance at all and now stood at the far end of what was apparently a control room—so incredibly huge that its ceiling and further wall were lost in a haze of distance.

And all about them crowded machines, reflecting the green light from a multitude of polished projections. And facing the wall through which they had come was a drum-like object, with a pale lavender beam just fading from it.

Then came a man of this strange race, attired from head to foot in a close-fitting costume, which shimmered like silver cloth.

This, with the all-prevalent green light—the source of which was a mystery—produced an eye-catching effect, even more so because of the man's vast size.

The Crusaders stared in awe at the colossus advancing towards them along one of the machine-gangways. When he eventually arrived at close quarters they had to crane their necks to see as far as his waistline. They estimated he was about thirty feet in height and proportionately broad, an immensity that made even Abna's seven feet of height seem insignificant.

Evidently the giant was in the midst of appraisement for he made no communication for a moment or two. As he stooped forward his face was visible, filling all the "sky." On the whole it was a pleasant though determined face, high-foreheaded, and topped with a shock of white hair. The Amazon in particular noticed that upon his tunic, at chest level, there reposed a small instrument that could have been a microphone or some such gadget.

"Now, my friends, we meet..." The words were clear enough but they boomed and rolled like thunder through the vast reaches.

"I bid you welcome, Golden Amazon of Earth, Abna of Jupiter, Viona, and Mexone. I trust my words are intelligible to you: this instrument I am wearing should alter the speed of the sound waves to make my voice sensible to your ears."

"We understand perfectly," the Amazon said, feeling somewhat overawed by the gigantic size of the man. "Whom are we addressing? From where do you come?"

"My name is Lixom, and I am the commander of this vessel. My home planet, and that of my comrades, is outside this space. Its name is Dra, if it be that such a fact interests you."

"It does interest us," the Amazon said. "You say your world is outside this space... Would I be correct if I said it is in a supra-universe beyond this one?"

"You would be correct. In the normal order of things this universe of yours is but a molecule on our world, such is the strange relation of cosmic sizes. Supra-universes and micro-universes exist side by side. Naturally, in order to come into this universe we have reduced our size, and our vessel, to the limit of safety—but even now, to judge from yourselves, we are of abnormal size. No matter: we can still communicate."

There was a pause for a moment, then Lixom added, "I am not behaving entirely as a host should, my friends. I think we can converse in more comfortable quarters. Follow me, if you please."

He turned and walked up the aisle, a man as big as a good-sized house. The Crusaders looked at each other and hesitated; then Abna gave a shrug.

"We're in it: we might as well finish it."

So, together, they followed their enormous host between the fabulous machines and passed finally from the aisle-way into what was clearly an anteroom. There was furniture of sorts, all of it conforming to earthly standards, but so huge it was overpowering.

"If you will be seated, I will make arrangements for refreshment to be brought you," Lixom said, and with a huge sweep of his arm he indicated an object resembling a settee... But how to get on to it? This he solved in a moment by picking up the Amazon, Abna, Viona and Mexone each in turn, between finger and thumb, and placing them on the settee in a sitting position, exactly as a child might do with a tiny doll.

This done, he clapped his hands and the airwaves echoed with the reverberation. In response to his clap a woman entered, only slightly less tall than Lixom himself, and attired in a similar head to toe costume. What Lixom said was not clear since he talked in his normal speed, hut when he had finished the woman gazed towards the manikin Crusaders in a group on the settee and then turned and went out.

"Now, my friends..." Lixom seated himself in an armchair opposite and it became easier to study his face. He rested his elbows on his out-thrust knees and allowed Brobdingnagian hands to dangle down between them.

"Now, my friends, I believe we have information to exchange. First, let me tell you that I can, under effort, read thoughts—but this is an art that I do not practice to any extent because I believe the thoughts of an individual are sacrosanct and should not be probed except under necessity. With regard to yourselves, I consider that necessity to have arisen and as a result I know your names, your language, and your ambitions. Further than that I shall not probe since I am reasonably convinced you are not hostile. You merely seek to know what we are doing in your space, do you not?"

"We are very interested," the Amazon admitted. "From our thoughts you may have gathered that our chief purpose in life is the uplifting of the backward, ignorant planetary inhabitants, and because of that we wish to be sure that you have no ill purpose in being in our space."

"None at all, Golden Amazon. We are here for scientific reasons—of necessity indeed—and we have no evil designs towards anybody."

The man smiled—a vast, huge smile. For some reason it was not entirely convincing—at least not to the Amazon. She thought for a moment and then asked a question.

"Would I be going too far if I asked what your scientific necessity might he?"

The smile faded. "At the moment, Golden Amazon, I do not feel disposed to discuss it. Later perhaps, when we have become more intimately acquainted— Ah, here is your refreshment. I gave orders that it should be served on a small scale. I trust you will find it palatable."

The Crusaders said nothing. They watched as the gigantic serving girl reached down an, arm as thick as a tree trunk, holding out a golden dish of food in her colossal fingers. First she served the Amazon, then the others, standing by all the time to supply their smallest need. They ate—and drank—of the meaty food and wine-like liquor, remarking to themselves that both were extremely pleasant. Then at last the meal was over and the giantess collected the plates and tiny glasses in her tabletop hands and departed to regions unknown. Lixom watched her go and then resumed conversation.

"For your information, my friends, I think you

should know that any departure from this spaceship, now you are upon it, would not be—desirable. On the other hand, though we shall not release you, you are entitled to and shall have every comfort, respected for the scientists you are... You see—" He hesitated for a moment, surveying them with huge dark eyes—"it would hardly be of any benefit to you to return to a universe where nothing exists any more, would it? You are better alive, and useful to us."

"Where nothing exists any more?" the Amazon repeated, puzzled.

"I said I would tell you of our scientific necessity for being here when we became better acquainted, but thinking it over I do not see what there is to be gained by delay. You are here, and here you will stop. The issue is as simple as that... And of course you won't attempt to escape because, clever though your science is, it is not of the sane high order as our own. You do not, for instance, understand the full details of the fourth, fifth, and sixth dimensions, do you? The means by which you came aboard the ship, and also the means by which you were communicated with when the radio-television pickup entered your Ultra?"

It was on the tip of the Amazon's tongue to say that aboard the Ultra, if she could only get back to it, were many scientific devices, including Time-controllers and a Zero-Thought Amplifier, which could destroy anything material in existence—then she refrained. This was one of those cases where co-operation with the enemy—if enemy Lixon really was—might produce more results than direct antagonism.

"It would seem," she replied slowly, "that our science is indeed not of the same order as yours. It hurts to confess it, but apparently it is so."

The reply made Abna, Mexone and Viona, glance sharply; then they gathered the line the Amazon was taking and kept quiet.

As for Lixon, he seemed entirely satisfied with the situation.

"I will explain to you our purpose in being here, my friends, and you will see that we are not really hostile to anybody or anything in this universe of yours, but are here because science demands it... Now, to the main cause of our visit, which is linked completely with our own world in the supra-universe beyond. We have there a new system of atomic power, which we are perfecting. Whilst atomic power is nothing new to us in itself, the system to which we are applying it definitely is. That too need not concern you. Our trouble is that our atomic experiments are being balked by one flaw, one molecule... You understand me so far?"

"So far," the Amazon agreed, looking like a tiny but beautiful doll on the enormous settee.

"We have a special generator for our atomic work, and we are using ordinary water as our source of fuel, water that has been specially prepared and treated through many years to be of the exact qualify we desire. The water passes endlessly through the generator, and will do until all its atomic bases are converted into energy. By 'passing endlessly' I mean that the same body of water is used over and over again."

"That is understood," the Amazon said. "Some of our man-made fountains use the same principle, squirting the water forth and then using it again when it has passed through outlet and intake pipes."

"Quite so. Then you gather the principle. However, we have discovered a flaw. At a certain point in the water stream the atomic generator misses fire, and that could cause untold chaos when applied to the system we have in mind. We have made countless tests of the water—we wish to use no other for it is specially treated for our purpose, as I have said, and represents the work of years—and finally we were forced to a definite conclusion. One molecule in the water is not responsive—a rare thing, but it does happen sometimes. That means the molecule must be eliminated from the other molecules surrounding it."

The Amazon shrugged. "I should say that you are faced with an almost impossible task, due to the incredible smallness of a molecule for one thing, and the impossibility of isolating or eliminating it from the others. Even if it could be done with the precision instruments which you probably have, there would arise the danger of disrupting the other molecules in the immediate neighborhood."

"That is precisely our difficulty," Lixom agreed. "But we solved it finally by deciding to enter the offending molecule itself, and eliminate it from within, so to speak."

The Amazon gave a slight start. "You're not saying

that this universe of ours is the offending molecule?"

"I'm afraid I am saying just that." There was no expression on Lixom's face. "This is a universe for you: to us, just one molecule in multi-millions in a stream of prepared water on our own planet of Dra. Yes, this is the molecule we seek, and that is why we are here. On our own planet we entered our space ship—this one—and by reduction processes became small enough to enter the flowing water stream. Still smaller, and smaller, until we were small enough to enter the molecule itself. At that point we were within this universe—coming suddenly and almost magically within it as we were no longer large enough to exist in our own sphere and therefore automatically became a part of this one."

"Which explains your sudden appearance in this part of space," the Amazon mused. "We didn't quite understand how it all happened."

"Well you do now. We have discovered, since being here that elimination of this molecule from within presents no real problem. It can be done successfully with our instruments, and will occasion no harm to ourselves—or yourselves. When it is done—a matter of perhaps three years time—we'll return home with the problem solved."

"And this universe destroyed..." The Amazon looked at him with her unfathomable eyes. "You talk most glibly of destroying this molecule which is a universe. You are quite unconcerned about the untold billions of lives that will be snuffed out in the process."

The enormous shoulders moved in a shrug. "Golden Amazon, I believe you to be a realist, so look at it as we see it. If you had a magnificent achievement at stake and were balked in one small detail, what would you do? You'd remove the detail, obviously. If lives were to be sacrificed in the removal of that detail, where would be the use of being sentimental about it? All life must die some day: whether it comes sooner or later matters not. Better sooner if a great scientific triumph is to be accomplished."

CHAPTER 2

WILES OF THE AMAZON

The Amazon gave a slow, cynical smile. "And you assured us, Lixom, that you are not really hostile towards anybody in this universe! In view of what you've just said that's a little hard to believe!"

"Yet it is truth. We have no actual hostility, anymore than you would personally hate an army of ants. Yet, say, if the object they were tenanting caused you trouble in your experiments you would eliminate it, wouldn't you?"

"Yes..." The Amazon hesitated, momentarily catching Abna's eye. "Perhaps I should. One cannot progress without somebody getting hurt, it seems."

"Only too true, Amazon... Well, now, you will see why I say you must all stay here because you'll have nowhere to go anyway when our experiments are over. There will be no universe to which you can return."

The Amazon asked quietly, "You say three years for your experiment. Are you reckoning by our time standards or your own?"

"Yours... In fact the experiment has already begun.

It began when we first arrived. We knew exactly how we would set about the elimination of this molecule—this universe."

"You have...already begun?" the Amazon repeated slowly. "Would it be in order of I asked how you even start on such a vast task as eliminating a Universe?"

"It is not so very difficult, Amazon, but I think the full story can wait until later: my attention is needed elsewhere in this vessel at the moment." The giant rose to his feet and in one surging movement his head and shoulders become remote in the heights of the room. "I have said that from now on you are to consider yourselves as part of our own party henceforth providing—always providing—you do not give trouble. Which you hardly could do with your infinitesimal size, I imagine."

For a moment there was reverberating sardonic laughter. The Amazon felt herself grow hot with fury but she controlled herself and remained passive on the settee.

"Since you are part of our party I have given instructions that a room of normal dimensions be prepared to fit your small size. Elo, the female servant whom you saw a while ago, has had those details in hand, informing our scientists that certain portions of the ship have to be electronically reduced to suit you. I should imagine everything is now in order..."

There followed the thunderous handclap and presently the giantess known as Elo appeared. She advanced to her master, listened to his sonorous words, and then nodded her dark head quickly. Lixom turned on colossal feet.

"Everything is ready, my friends. If you will let Elo take charge of you everything will be in order. We will discuss again before long."

With that, Lixom departed from the anteroom, leaving the servant girl staring down at the settee in vague perplexity.

At that the Amazon stirred, slipped over the edge of the settee, and landed lightly on the floor. Abna, Mexone, and Viona quickly followed her, then they all four stood gazing up at the feminine mountain as she loomed over them. It seemed in her mind to speak, then, evidently realizing the difficulties she thought better of it and instead motioned that she was to be followed.

Her journey led from the anteroom, down a corridor as vast as the interior of a cathedral, and finally to one of many doors which had obviously been quickly reduced in size to suit the Crusaders' proportions. Elo indicated it, stooped and opened it—as though she were a very big girl playing with a doll's house—then she stood aside to let the four pass. They entered a comparatively normal room, then turned sharply as the door closed abruptly behind them. There was the sound of a catch snapping into place.

"So here we are," the Amazon commented grimly. "And from the general aspect of things we'll stay here!"

Abna did not answer her immediately. With Viona and Mexone he was glancing about the room, noting its various appointments.

It left nothing to be desired. Beds, furniture, concealed green lighting, soft carpets—and even a window disguised with curtains, actually a porthole, looking out on the deeps of space.

"Well, now what?" Viona asked, moving forward and sprawling her lithe young body in one of the huge armchairs. "On the one hand Big Boy Lixom doesn't seem to dislike us, yet on the other he's our enemy. What do we make of the situation?"

"At the moment, nothing," the Amazon said, glancing about her. Then by way of further explanation she took a small memo pad of metal fooling from her belt and stenciled on it quickly. Finally she held it up so the others could see what she had written—"Beware of microphones and tele-pickups. We will communicate by writing."

"Good idea," Abna said, and pulled his own memo pad from his belt.

Thereafter they began a totally silent exchange of views on the situation as they found it, the upshot of which was that they all agreed that Lixom had no personal resentment towards them, but was more or less compelled to "immobilize" them from further activity because of the schemes in which he was involved.

In a sense, he was a friendly enemy, with no compunction whatever about eliminating the Earth-Universe so long as his own scientific object was achieved.

The immediate and absorbing problem that faced the four was how to defeat the Colossus of Dra in his grandiose scheme and yet retain their own lives. Obviously, he must not be allowed to complete his plan of eliminating the molecule called a universe—yet with no weapons of any vital value, and cut off from the Ultra, faced with a scientist of considerable skill and, if necessary, telepathic powers by which he could anticipate their moves, how were the four to start?

"For the moment," the Amazon wrote, "we are at a dead end. The slightest miscalculation on our part will cost us our lives. I can foresee only one possible way of making an opposing start against Lixom, and that is to co-operate with him."

Abna: "Co-operate with him? How can one cooperate with a man who has captured us, whose avowed intention is to destroy the universe to which we belong?"

Amazon: "We are at a loss at the moment because we don't know what methods he is using to achieve his object. He said he would explain that later, and because I think he wishes to be friendly—all other considerations apart—I think he will do as he says. Once we know what he is doing, and his method, we are in a position to attack his weak links. There must be some somewhere. Until the chance arises to get the information we want we must behave as friends and attempt nothing drastic."

Viona: "That will be hard work for you, mother. You like action—sudden, violent, and decisive."

Amazon: "I know. And later on I'll get it... All right then, for the time being we speak of only normal things, flatter Lixom in every way possible, and get to know what we want."

The decision made, the Amazon put her notepad away, and gave a meaning nod to the others. Silent and thoughtful they crossed to the window and peered between the curtains on the velvet blackness of space. In the illimitable distance blazed and glittered the glory of the Milky Way. To the four—a universe; *their* universe. To the giant who held them in his power, a molecule causing trouble in his own far-off titanic world of Dra...

"Can't see the Ultra from here," Mexone commented finally; and the Amazon shrugged.

"No. For one thing this ship is of enormous size, and for another I estimate that we've turned a corner or two in our travels since we entered it. Presumably the Ultra's still where we left it, magnetically anchored to the side."

"Maybe we'd employ the time usefully if we had a rest," Abna commented. "We don't know what we may called upon to do later and reserves of strength are always useful."

His suggestion was adopted, chiefly because there was nothing else to do. Much though inactivity irked them they had to accept it—at least for the moment, but when it went on day after day—as measured by their watches that is—they began to become irritated and nearly forgot their plan of friendly co-operation with their captor. They felt that they were being forced to keep out of the way whilst necessary scientific experiments proceeded, and this was probably correct. At times they heard deep throbbing sounds of power from somewhere in the vessel, and it was certainly not the spaceship itself on the move for space and the stars remained unchanged. The spaceship was motionless, or comparatively, its only movement being produced by the radiations of space, which shifted it slightly as waves shift an anchored boat.

Meals, rest periods, sleep, pointless conversation, occasional prowling round the room in which they were kept: this was the lot of the quartet for nearly a week of Earth-time, which tried their patience beyond endurance. Then, at long last, there came a break in the deadly monotony: their room door opened and the stooping form of the woman Elo was visible beyond. She spoke in sepulchral, dragging tones.

"My...maaasssterrr...wa...aa...its...to...speee-aaak."

"About time," the Amazon muttered, hurrying to the doorway. "Now maybe we can get a bit of action."

The others followed her past the giantess, then waited as she crushed past them and went ahead down the corridor, acting in her usual capacity as guide. Following her, the four could not help but remark that for all her thirty-odd feet of height she had a definite grace and a shapely body, clearly revealed by the head-to-toe one piece garment she wore, whether she had strength to match her size was a debatable point.

So, presently, into the huge control room where the adventure had started. Lixom was there, attired as usual in his superb silver-cloth tunic. He inclined his faraway white head as the four became apparent to him.

"A pleasure to see you again, my friends." He gestured briefly and the woman Elo departed. "I felt it was time I had more words with you—mainly to tell you what I have decided."

"Decided?" the Amazon repeated. "There is hardly any question of that, is there? You have decided to eliminate this molecule called a universe, and we are compelled to throw in our lot with yours. What more is there?"

"There is the matter of making sure that your connivance with us is complete, my friends. There will always be a doubt about that as long as your spaceship remains so close, attached to our own vessel."

"It is of no use to us," the Amazon shrugged. "We cannot get at it. We don't know how to leave this vessel of yours, and we don't understand the fourth dimensional trick that would enable us to pass through the wall. So, as far as we are concerned, our Ultra might as well not exist."

"So you call it the Ultra? Meaning par excellence, I assume?" There was a brief pause as the dark eyes became brooding. "You have named it well. I have examined it and it contains many instruments and weapons of far reaching power. One in particular, which, as far as I can gather, is able to transform anything material into a non-existent state. That is clever—rather too clever if one has one's safety to reckon with."

The Amazon said: "Obviously you're referring to the Zero-Thought Amplifier. Yes, it's one of our most powerful weapons, but I might as well tell you here and now that, come what may, we don't intend to reveal its secret."

"I wouldn't wish you, to, Golden Amazon. Our science has no need of a secret like that. With our dimensional knowledge we can dispose of anything unsavory at a moment's notice. But on the other hand an instrument like that operates in a way foreign to our science so I have decided to be rid of it, along with the other machines which the Ultra possesses."

"You mean…destroy the Ultra?" Mexone demanded.

"Not destroy it. Examination has shown that it has a composition of interlocked atoms, which it would demand the ultimate of power to unlock. We do not feel disposed to use so much power for such a purpose when there is a simpler way."

"And what's that?" the Amazon snapped, unable to control the frustrated fury she was experiencing.

"Time, Golden Amazon—Time. I noticed from the instruments aboard the Ultra that you know something of the laws of Time. That doesn't really signify but it will help you to understand that sending your Ultra into a past Time where it can be of no use to you is not impossible. Much easier than trying to destroy it."

"But you can't do that!" Viona burst out; then the sudden raising of Lixom's voice drowned her out.

"Don't tell me, Viona, what I can do or not do! I am doing it—now! You may care to watch."

Switches snapped abruptly under the giant's hands and a television screen came to life in the wall. The quartet was forced to watch with mixed feelings as they saw the outside of the giant spaceship with the Ultra clinging to it. Then presently the Ultra detached itself slightly but still remained close to the giant vessel. Very gradually the Ultra began to grow misty, transparent, and then was gone.

"My regrets, my friends," Lixom said gravely. "I have sent that vessel of yours many centuries back into Time—a complete vanishing act. It was not as swift a disappearance as I would have liked because actually I haven't the available power to spare. However, the machine will move gradually into past Time and cease to be of concern to you. We need all the power we have for other projects... Since the Ultra is now in a past time it will never again be of any use to you."

The Amazon looked at the screen, at the void into which the Ultra had vanished, then she gave a sigh. By an enormous effort she controlled herself. She fought down the desire to lash out left and right at the gigantic scientist for the thing he had done. Evidently he made one of those rare attempts to read her thoughts for suddenly he laughed—that gusty, reverberating laugh that rolled heavily through the air.

"Again I can only express my regrets for the actions which necessity compels," he said. "I am sure now that you will be with us with complete unity. So to other things. I promised upon your first arrival, that in time I would reveal to you, how the elimination of this universe-molecule is to be brought about. You are still interested?"

"Very," the Amazon said, in a hard, brittle voice.

"So be it then. You are aware, naturally, of the theory of the expanding Universe?"

"Of course," the Amazon assented. "That the universe is still expanding outwards from the initial explosion of cosmic force which created it. That isn't a theory, Lixom: it is a fact. We've been to the outermost edges of the Universe and we know that the explosion is a definite thing."

"Good. Then appreciate this: The reverse order of an explosion is an implosion, by which an explosion is returned to its original state. Correct?"

The Amazon nodded slowly, her keen mind searching round the scientific postulations.

"The matter is comparatively simple, as I said at first." Lixom spread his enormous hands. "We have the mastery of Time and dimensions, as you have already seen. We have only to reverse the order of Time prevalent in this Universe to cause it, so to speak, to turn back on itself. Hence the explosion no longer exists. It is implosion, sweeping backwards to the original core where it will finally meet extinction because then it will have reached the point where it didn't even exist."

"Complete, absolute elimination," Abna muttered. "We can see now what you mean. But surely this backward time movement of the entire universe incorporates everything in it, including this spaceship of yours?"

"Not necessarily. This ship is, so to speak, isolated in the general reverse movement—or at least it will be when the time comes. As yet we are only operating the backward time effect on the far edges of the universe. According to our calculations it will be five or more years before our task is accomplished. Last time we conversed I said three: later postulations say at least five. Things are not progressing as rapidly as we had expected."

"Then in that five years," the Amazon said slowly, "this reverse process which is now on the fringes of the Universe will creep gradually nearer this isolated spaceship of yours?"

"Exactly—moving faster as the circumference of reversal moves inwards. Obviously the circle will be smaller. Here—see for yourselves the beginning of the process."

Lixom turned once again to his switch panel and depressed several buttons. As a result a telescopic-reflector screen came into action, picturing some distant portion of the universe. For several seconds the quartet stood watching distant stars ceasing to be before what seemed to be a tide of darkness. Actually it was not that. Space was unchanged, but the material units in it—in this case stars—were rapidly being returned to their primal state of non-existence.

"Very interesting," the Amazon commented grimly, as Lixom switched off. "Even so we do not as yet understand how you, do it. At a rough guess I'd say you're using something of a dimensional nature."

"Your guess would be correct, Golden Amazon. Stated mathematically, Time is the fifth dimension. The other four are length, breadth, thickness, and space. However, the backward or forward progress of Tine is easily controllable through the fifth dimension, but it demands enormous reserves of power—which are now at work, at least on the most distant points of this molecule universe. I do not expect you to understand our science, since it is so far ahead of yours, but I can at least give you a theory which might explain our method."

"Please do," the Amazon invited, alert for every detail.

"It is difficult to find illustration," Lixom mused. "Maybe I should take space and distance as an example. Imagine a distant world, then imagine it viewed through a telescope. That world comes nearer to the eye, doesn't it?"

"Apparently it does," the Amazon corrected. "The world under observation isn't really any closer: it is only the combination of lenses which make it appear so."

"Exactly so, but the fact remains even if it is an abstract one. So it is with Time. Time's normal process is to advance, but by a scientific process—as abstract as that of a world viewed through a telescope—that Time can be reversed, and the material things within it forced to retrace to their original nothingness. You can produce the same effect by running a length of moving picture film backwards, but whereas you do it only with photographs we do it in fact. That is where the abstruse state of a fifth dimension comes in. It is beyond living brains to grasp it and requires machines to analyze its operation in detail."

"So be it," the Amazon shrugged. "The fact remains that you can do it, and there is nothing we can do about it… But you surely don't do it alone? Up to now we have only seen two people aboard this vessel—yourself and the woman Elo. I assume that there are others?"

"Definitely. Trained scientists by the score—men and women, all devoted to the task upon which we are working. This ship is divided into different sections of which this control room is exclusively my own. In other parts there are the machine rooms—where the backward time effect is produced—the living quarters, the main control hall for controlling this vessel, the provision departments, scientific laboratories, and so forth. This vessel is, in fact, a scientific city in itself."

Viona said: "You seem to have different light for different places. We noticed golden, green, and sapphire-lighted portholes. Any particular reason?"

"Yes, there's a reason. The eyes of the Draian race vary a great deal in color-receptivity. In certain colors they give the maximum efficiency, so our people are graded into different light-compartments according to the nature of their tasks. I, for instance, am most at home in green light—but perhaps you may not be. What is your preferred color?"

"Golden," the Amazon answered, after a moment.

"Very well. I will see to it the golden light is used

henceforth in your private apartments. I regret you have had to tolerate green so far…"

There was silence for a moment. The Amazon stood thinking something out, and Abna, Viona, and Mexone, accustomed to her every mood, guessed—correctly— that something was about to happen. Lixom waited too, quite patiently, apparently ready to answer whatever further questions might be put to him.

"You spoke of special machine rooms which produce the Time-reversal effect on the far edges of the Universe…" the Amazon said at length, and as Lixom nodded his huge head she went on, "As a scientist, and one forced to live in association with you, I would rather like to see these machine rooms. Would that be possible?"

"Might I ask why, Golden Amazon?"

The Amazon raised her shoulders negatively, deliberately masking her thoughts in case the giant decided to read them.

"I merely thought you might grant that favor. Obviously we can't do any harm, and to such as us inactivity is intolerable. For myself I would rather like to see a concrete demonstration of what you have tried to outline to us in theory. If I have trespassed too far in asking, I apologize."

The immense scientist did not respond immediately. He turned his back and went to the huge window, gazing out onto space as he evidently tried to come to a decision. The Amazon gave the others a glance, a glance sufficient to show that she had started some subtle and none too obvious campaign of her own.

Finally Lixon turned again, his dark eyes looking at the four each in turn. "I see nothing against granting your request. Come with me."

He led the way out of the control room and thence through various regions of the colossal ship and so finally into the green-lighted immensity of the Time-controlling machine room. In a moment the four recognized it as the same room they had seen from the Ultra when they had originally tried to examine the great spaceship.

"I have not the tine to personally escort you," Lixom said. "You are at perfect liberty to look and study as you wish." He paused and then added quietly, "I do not have to emphasize that you must conduct yourselves with…restraint."

Then he had gone again, enormous doors of metal swinging shut behind him. The quartet looked at each other, feeling indescribably tiny and insignificant in this behemoth place of titanic machines and brooding, watching scientists.

Abna suddenly clenched his fists. "If we were amongst people on a par with us for size we'd feel happier. Anyway, I would. They're all so colossal. We just can't start anything, Vi, if that's what you're thinking."

She glanced about her. "I think we can talk safely for a moment," she said, without looking at Abna. "It's unlikely that hidden mikes are in here, though hidden television may be. Anyway, we've got this far. Right into the heart of things."

Viona gave a sigh and rubbed her coppery hair perplexedly. "In the heart of things to what end?" she demanded. "I feel as though I'm standing in the middle of the most complicated clock ever made."

The Amazon did not answer her. She was surveying the myriad huge machines, and the dozens of men in silvery head-to-toe tights at work on them.

"Here is the heart of the whole business," she said finally. "In all fairness to Lixom, we have to admit that he's only attempting a scientific experiment to make his own science perfect on distant Dra. But for us, inhabitants of the universe he's trying to eliminate, it's different. We've got to stop him—and we're never going to do it by listening to his scientific theories which haven't one ring of conviction about them."

"You mean he isn't speaking the truth?" Mexone asked.

"I mean he didn't give anything away. He gave us a theory, but one can't destroy a mere theory. We want the actual know-how of this Time-controlling system, and this is the place to get it. I don't think these scientists will be as guarded as Lixom. I'm even surprised he allowed us to come here, and I can only assume he did so because he's satisfied we can't do anything."

"In which he was correct, I'm afraid," Viona said dubiously.

"That remains to he seen. Anyway, we can at least try to stop things, even if we sacrifice ourselves in the process. We've no way out with the Ultra, gone, so the obvious course is to put a spoke in Lixom's wheel before things go too far. Come—let's see what we can do."

Abna dropped a hand to his instrument belt, his fingers closing over the butt of his protonic gun. The Amazon gave him a look.

"Not very wise, Abna. We're peaceful investigators, supposed to be. When a chance comes I'll give the signal. Right?"

"Okay," Abna shrugged. "But with people this size it seems to me that protonic guns are the only things that will make sense."

"Which, from you, surprises me," the Amazon commented. "We might even use hypnotism, where the size of the people is of no consequence."

There the brief argument ended and the Amazon singled out the scientist who, from his isolated position at a huge controlling panel, seemed to be "overseer." She approached him with a smile, and when she wished it so the Amazon's smile could be very bewitching indeed.

"Is it possible," she asked the giant, gazing at his silver-clad figure as he sat on a curious kind of stool, "for you and I to hold an intelligent conversation, due to our different voice speeds? As you may know, we have become compatriots of yours due to force of circumstances, and Lixom gave us permission to study this powerhouse as we wished."

Silence for a moment. Abna looked at Viona and Mexone and read astonishment akin to his own. It was rarely indeed that the Amazon subdued her efficient, scientific personality in order to become a natural woman—and exert all the subtle influence and charm that were the prerogative of her sex.

The giant looked reflective for a moment, weighing up the slender, beautifully modeled woman standing so small facing him. Finally he took an instrument from a pocket in his tunic and fastened it on his huge chest. It was immediately obvious as being the same kind of instrument Lixom used as a minute transformer for reconciling the length of sound waves.

"I see no reason why an intelligent conversation should not be held, Golden Amazon," he responded. "Lixom has already told me about you and the others with you. I hope I can extend every courtesy to you as visitors from another world."

"Prisoners, you mean," Mexone growled; then anything more he night have said was silenced by the stony look the Amazon gave him. But she was again all smiles as she turned back to the scientist.

"Our science," she said almost apologetically, "is of an order so far behind yours that we don't understand one thing about it. In a moment of over-confidence I asked Lixom to outline to me how you manage to contract this universe-molecule back to its original size. He explained everything in terms of Time and dimensions, but I didn't understand a word he said. Finally I asked him if we could view the powerhouse for ourselves, and he consented. So here we are… I feel sure that you, not having the high office of Lixom, will be more inclined to explain things to a rather stupid woman like myself."

"Stupid!" Abna muttered to Viona. "Great cosmos, what next?"

"This," Viona murmured, "is the process known as wheedling. Being a woman myself I recognize it, but I never thought mother was capable of it!"

"She's a woman after all," Abna, commented wryly. "Though I do agree one is inclined to forget it some-times..."

"I will explain things as well as I can," the foreman-scientist smiled. "What particularly do you want to know?"

"Oh, just exactly how you do it," the Amazon smiled.

"Time," the scientist said, "is related to the fifth dimension. It progresses onwards like a river, but because it is time it is also interlinked with space. You cannot move in tine without moving in space. Clear so far?"

"Clear so far," the Amazon agreed.

"Let us return to the river analogy. If you had the power to tilt the ground over an infinite distance you could force a river to flow back whence it had come, could you, not?"

"Turn back on itself? Yes, it could be done."

"Very well then. Imagine space to be the ground. That is as near as I can picture it for you because of the difficulty of explaining the fifth dimension. We, so to speak, are using forces which tilt space and cause the movement of Time to move backwards, instead of in its normal forward progress."

Viona, listening intently, was just about to say that the system was nothing like the Time-control on the Ultra, then, just on the verge of speaking she checked herself.

"And how do you 'tilt' space?" the Amazon asked. "As a scientist myself, though not a very good one, I would like to see it in operation."

"I can give you an idea of what happens." The giant rose from his seat. "Come with me…"

He led the way down the aisle-way amongst the machines and the four followed him with surprising meekness, three of them at least not quite sure even now what the Amazon was driving at.

Finally they arrived at an isolated unit that had all the appearance of a big generator, the one peculiar thing about it being a funnel-projection at one end which directly faced a specially contrived opening in the laboratory wall.

"This," the scientist said, "is one of the twenty four Time-reversing projectors, fully in operation. You notice that its radiation is given an unhindered path into space. That clear space you see in the spaceship wall is actually a special transparent substance, which is not affected by the radiations, otherwise—like everything else in front of this projector's influence—it would be transported into past time. Quite obviously, we have to keep the spaceship sealed against the void of space, yet allow free passage of these radiations to the ends of the universe. Is that clear?"

"Perfectly." The Amazon surveyed the monster generator and then looked up at the huge funnel and the clear space in front of it. Suddenly she took something from her belt—a small adjustable spanner, and weighed it in her hand.

"If you wish to test the efficiency of the projector, by all means do," the foreman smiled.

She nodded and then tossed the spanner into the area of the projector funnel. The spanner dropped to the floor, but it was well within the projector's influence. There was something uncanny about the way the spanner went misty, then transparent, and finally disappeared altogether.

"It has gone into past time," the scientist explained. "The space around it was turned back on itself, preventing time from going forward in the normal way. Maybe you have some idea now of the process..."

"Enough anyway," the Amazon said, thinking about something. "And there are twenty three other projectors like this at work?"

"That is so, located at various points in a circle around this machine room. Being in a circle they can project their influence to all points of this universe-molecule."

"Wonderful! Truly wonderful," the Amazon said. "You've been most helpful. At least I now understand a little more of what is being attempted... Tell me, how do you manage to reduce things in size? I mean, how did you arrange to reduce our personal chambers to a size befitting our smaller size?"

Abna frowned as he listened. The Amazon knew quite well that size could be governed by widening or contracting the electronic orbits of the mass to be altered. Such a device existed—or had existed—on the Ultra before its "banishment" into Time and space. Why, then, should she seek to know the answer to something she thoroughly understood?

"The matter was not difficult," the foreman-scientist said, obviously flattered at the constant call on his knowledge. "Let me show you. Here—this way."

Again he preceded the four through a wilderness of machinery until he came a big device on pneumatic wheels. On the exterior it was a mass of dials and complicated controls.

"We reduce or increase anything with the aid of this," he explained. "Any material mass is composed of electronic orbits, like planets whirling round a sun. Contract the orbits, and naturally the mass grows smaller. Increase, and it becomes larger. However, the mass-weight does not remain the same…it decreases or increases proportionately because the type of energy we use also affects gravity—"

"That we know already," Mexone said. "We have had such a device on the Ultra. For—" His voice suddenly broke into a gasp as Abna gave him a sharp kick on the ankle.

"Shut up," Abna hissed under his breath. "Let Vi do the talking. She knows what she's doing."

Mexone grunted something and became silent again as the Amazon looked at him. The scientist looked too, obviously puzzled.

"Why," he asked, "should you wish to know the details of a system which is already clear to you, Amazon?"

"I was just seeing if, in some respects, your science was like our own," she responded blandly; then before the scientist could sort her statement out she hurried on, "You have been most kind showing us everything, but there is still something which worries me."

"And what is that, Amazon?"

"You have twenty four time projectors in operation. What would happen if one of them failed to function? Would that in any way affect things?"

The scientist hesitated for a moment as though a vague suspicion of this blandly charming woman had crossed his mind; then he shrugged off the suspicion and answered her.

"Yes, it definitely would affect things. The retrogression of Time must be a continuous thing when applied to the Universe-molecule. The machines are all interlocked in their action, and one out of step with the others would cause serious trouble in our experiments. That is why these technicians are working here, all of them keeping each machine to a millionth degree of perfection, ceaselessly. Relays of technicians will be at the task for the estimated five years it will take for the task to be completed."

"Such wonderful organization," the Amazon smiled. "I could almost forget the destruction you are causing in admiration for your scientific skill."

The scientist said nothing. He fancied that for a moment he glimpsed another side to the Amazon—a hardening of her beautiful face, a glitter in her deep purple eyes. But in manner she seemed unchanged, still conveying that suggestion of rather bemused femininity. As for Abna, Viona, and Mexone, they were completely lost. They had no idea even now what the Amazon was attempting to do—if anything. But she knew her object, very much so. It was only a question of how and when to act. For a moment or two she stood thinking things out, her eyes on the distant machine-technicians at their posts.

CHAPTER 3

MICROSCOPIC SABOTEURS

"Would it be possible," the Amazon asked finally, as the scientist stood waiting, "To have one more look at the projector you showed us? I want to check on something, then I shall not need to bother you again…would you mind?"

"I would be only too pleased, if it helps to further your appreciation of our science." With that the huge scientist turned and led the way back towards the isolated region where the one huge projector stood. The Amazon fell into step with Abna, Viona, and Mexone as they followed him.

"What's the idea of all this?" Abna demanded, with faint irritation. "What are you driving at?"

"You'll see in a moment. The time for action is about here but I wanted to get one or two facts clear in my mind first… The most significant thing is that one of these projectors out of action upsets the rest of them."

"What about it? You don't imagine we can deal with projectors of this size, do you? Especially with armies of technicians around us."

"We can do a good deal— Quiet! He's looking at us."

They ceased talking as the foreman-scientist, still faintly suspicious, glanced back at them as he progressed. Whether or not he had Lixom's ability to read thoughts they did not know—but in any case they all automatically blanked their minds. At least the Amazon did. The others were so baffled it hardly mattered whether their thoughts were read or not.

So they again reached the isolated region where the giant projector stood. The Amazon surveyed the vast machine, and the foreman scientist, a little in front of her, raised a quizzical eyebrow.

"Do you seek further information, Amazon?" he asked.

"No, I don't think so..." The Amazon wandered closer to him—then suddenly, before there was the least chance to grasp what was intended, she hurtled herself forward. Though she was a mere doll in size compared to the enormous scientist, she had nevertheless her superhuman strength to aid her. It was her muscles that gave her the power for the original catapult leap; it was again her muscles that sent the scientist staggering backwards. His size did not matter when he was caught off balance by a hurtling body.

Unable to save himself he toppled backwards on his heels, and he had not the chance to recover as the Amazon's fists, small though they seemed, cracked savagely on his chin. In a couple of seconds he had reeled into the area of the projector funnel, and that was where the Amazon stopped, on the fringe of the influence emanating from the machine. She stared fixedly at the giant scientist as he made an effort to save himself. He got to his knees, becoming misty as he did so—but long before he had risen to his feet he had disappeared. Disturbed airwaves passed and that was all.

The Amazon relaxed slowly and glanced about her. The technicians were too far away to have noticed anything unusual in those hectic seconds... Abna came slowly forward and caught the Amazon's arm.

"What was the idea of that?" he demanded. "You realize what you've done, don't you?"

"Of course. I shouldn't have done it otherwise. I have dispatched our mountainous friend to somewhere in past time. Don't you see why? If I'd left him as he was he could have reported everything he's done and shown us to Lixom, and then there'd be trouble. As it is we've got freedom for a moment."

"Freedom to do what?" Viona demanded.

"To start the wrecking of these projectors—or at least one of them, which will put the others out of step."

"How?" Abna was looking justifiably bewildered.

"In the past we have had occasion to resort to infinite smallness to achieve our object: this time we look like having to do it again. Only difference this time is that the dangers are far greater and we've no Ultra to escape to even if we succeed. In other words," the Amazon finished, "we're going to gamble everything we've got, including our lives, in an effort to stop this universal elimination Lixom is attempting. You're with me, of course?"

Abna, Viona, and Mexone nodded slowly each in turn.

"Of course," Abna agreed. "But it would help if we knew what we're supposed to be doing. I can't see how—"

"Listen. I had that foreman-scientist show me where the size-controlling machine is for one good reason— so we'll know where to get at it. Fundamentally it has the same principle as the machine on our Ultra, and for that the cosmos be praised. We shouldn't have much difficulty in controlling it, and those technicians are far enough away not to cause us any trouble at the moment."

"And what happens when Lixom realizes we've disappeared?" Mexone demanded.

"We'll leave him to worry about that. Once we achieve microscopic size he'll have a hard job finding us... Now come on."

The Amazon moved purposefully, the others beside her. In a matter of moments they reached the intricate instrument that the foreman-scientist had said was the device for making any object smaller or larger by control of the electron orbits. The Amazon gave herself up to a study of the controls, which she could just reach. She was not bothered by the thought of any trouble at the moment. For one thing the technicians were at a good distance, and since they had seen the foreman scientist showing the quartet the various instruments they had no reason as yet to suspect anything unusual.

"This shouldn't be difficult," the Amazon said finally, her appraisement complete. "The system's practically the same as our own. Who's going to be the first to try?"

"Take me," Abna said, stepping into line with the device's output lens. "I'll risk it…"

The Amazon studied the controls again then switched on the power. She was rewarded by a deep humming note.

"So far so good," she murmured. "Once we've found the size we're going to adopt I can use the automatic control. That will take care of Viona, Mexone, and myself all at once. You're just a guinea pig for the moment, Abna. I suggest a sixteenth of an inch for height. Agreed?"

"Agreed," Abna assented, and stood waiting.

More adjustments. Finally the size was set on the scale reading and the Amazon pulled the switch that she assumed controlled operations, anxiously watching Abna meanwhile. Almost immediately he began to shrink gradually, and painlessly, as the electronic orbits forming the molecules of his body gradually contracted.

From his point of view the Amazon slowly assumed truly vast proportions as she stood by the machine, and by the time the shrinkage was complete Abna found himself looking only at two colossal golden shoes with flat rubber soles, the Amazon's usual footwear when clad in her black skin-tight costume…

Abna smiled to himself, a, speck amidst machines as large as the most towering mountains. He was not particularly afraid of the condition since he had experienced it before in other cosmic experiences: he was merely amused by the relative change in outlook now he stood a microscopic sixteenth of an inch in height.

Then, one by one, the others stepped into line—Viona, Mexone, and the Amazon, mighty living statues from Abna's point of view.

Somewhere in the heights the machine continued its functions and the three sank rapidly to Abna's own size, and there stopped its influence. The only thing apparent now was that all four were of the same height, a sixteenth of an inch, but to each other they all seemed to be identically level.

"Now what?" Abna asked, looking at the hummocks and depressions in the metal floor—actually tiny imperfections no bigger than a pinhead.

"Now for the difficult part," the Amazon said. "To all intents and purposes we are so small as to be invisible, so we don't have to exercise any particular caution in that respect. Our next job is to somehow climb into the works of that isolated Time-controlling projector and upset its operations. It lies over there."

She pointed into a blurred haze of latticed metalwork outlined against a cavernous green sky. Abna gave a puzzled look.

"How do you know it does? I see no sign of it."

"I took particular notice of the position before I shrank. Follow me: we'll cone to it in time."

They began moving, and it was surprising what a toilsome job it proved to be clambering over the imperfections and irregularities of the floor. Distances, too, were correspondingly increased to what they had been, with the result that it took them all of two hours to traverse the distance to the Time-controlling machine, a fantastic journey made through a wilderness of incomprehensible masses of looming metal—actually the legs and foundations of the countless machines.

"Right!" the Amazon paused, surveying the tremendous mountainside of metal that comprised the supports of the machine they wanted. "Somehow we're going to get in the interior. I should think one of the air grilles on the side would be the most likely bet."

She set the example and started climbing up the metalwork. Where she came to a sheer face she used mountaineering tactics and tough nylon rope from her belt pocket. Behind her came Abna, Viona, and Mexone, all of them rising higher and higher in the incredible gulf, until it seemed as though they were ascending the highest mountain in creation. The only point in their favor was that the air remained constant throughout, instead of becoming thinner as they rose, as would have been the case with a normal mountain.

With intervals for rest their ascent took them an hour. By this time they had come to a level plain—actually the metallic baseboard on which the projector's main bulk rested. They stopped to survey, and particularly the abyss below from which they had come.

"When we're inside the thing," the Amazon said,

indicating the big horizontal openings that constituted the air-intake grilles of the thing, "we'll really step into danger. We don't know what sort of electrical stuff we'll be involved in, but so long as we wreck it that's the main point. And we've got guns with which to do that."

She slapped the weapons on her belt, gave a grim smile, then jerked her head. A normal observer looking on would—if he possessed keen eyesight—have seen four microscopic figures creeping along like ants to the air grille of the huge projector, climb to the lowest one, and then disappear inside.

Inside the apparatus the four found everything more or less dark. What light there was consisted of the usual green, filtering through the grille slots, which put them in a more or less bilious-looking twilight. Nevertheless it was sufficient to see by... And what a vision they beheld! Wires everywhere, seeming as thick as cables, twining and snaking to a myriad different contacts. There were machine assemblies too, great cogs fitting within each other and turning slowly. Then the floor on which they stood was more or less a mat of wires, instead of being solid substance. And through the whole mad setup there throbbed a note of power.

"Where do we start?" Abna inquired.

"That's what we have to find out," the Amazon responded, looking at the wilderness of wiring. "Our job is to find a vital wire and destroy it—" She paused, then suddenly pointed. "That one for instance—thicker than the rest. It's probably supplying vital power. We can soon find out."

She pulled her proton gun from her belt, sighted it, and pressed the button. A jet of livid violet fire shot towards the chosen wire and smoke began to rise as tremendous heat ate at the insulation. It was must have been enormously tough since, usually, things just disappeared before the power of the protonic gun, volatized instantly. This time the process was slower, but it was effective just the same.

The insulation melted in great bubbling drops of waxy substance, which fell to the enigmas of wire lower in the machine. Finally the bare wire itself appeared. There was an abrupt blinding flash and explosion. Probably it was no more than a fuse, but with their sixteenth-inch size the Crusaders suffered the effects of major blast. They reeled back onto their "floor" of wires, dazzled and shaken.

It was as they gradually recovered from the shock that they became aware of something: the hum of power which had been all around them had ceased!

"I believe we've done it," the Amazon murmured, thrusting her gun back into her belt. "We've stopped this machine anyway—and the moment they've found the damage and try to repair it we'll shatter it again, or maybe go to another machine and shatter that."

"It won't be easy finding one of the other projectors at our present size," Viona commented. "We don't even know where they are!"

The Amazon reflected. "Mmm, that's a point. All right, we'll stay here as long as possible and wreck things every time they repair it. The longer we keep up the disorganization the more desperate things will become for them. That foreman scientist was quite certain that there had to be an uninterrupted flow of power—"

"Listen!" Mexone interrupted suddenly, holding up his hand for silence; and instantly the others froze to attention.

There was a strange sound in the enormous laboratory beyond. It seemed to have a rising and falling note and sounded exactly like thunder, yet it had not quite the same persistency of reverberation. For quite a time the four listened to it, their brows knitted in puzzlement; then suddenly the Amazon snapped her fingers.

"I've got it! Voices. Excited voices. Even in the ordinary way these folks sound like an avalanche when they talk: now we're even smaller the effect will be heightened. They're talking amongst themselves and coming this way…"

She moved forward along the wire matting floor and peered through the slot of the ventilator grille. There was a chaotic vision beyond—vast figures moving urgently amidst dense clouds of smoke, from the midst of which came the thunderous chorus of voices.

"What goes on?" Abna asked, coming to the Amazon's side, and she grinned in triumph.

"Trouble for the big boys apparently. I can't sum things up very well because of the size of everything, but at a rough guess I'd say that we've caused quite a deal of trouble by stopping this machine. It looks as though several of the others have short-circuited or caught fire in consequence. If so, all the better. Come to think of it, that's the right answer. The foreman said all the machines were interlocked. One going wrong would affect the lot! This, Abna, promises to be interesting."

Abna nodded, watching intently. Mexone and Viona moved in too and stood watching the panorama of smoke and giantism being enacted outside. Definitely there was serious trouble, and so far as could be judged valiant efforts were being made to rectify it.

"And that's only the beginning," the Amazon commented, giving Abna a glance. "They'll get everything straight, repair this machine, then we'll wreck it again for them!"

"Say—look!" Viona exclaimed abruptly, pointing behind and below.

For a second or two the others could hardly believe what they saw. Not far from them were rapidly developing flames, sweeping up from the underside of the machine, probably started by the lumps of boiling insulation that had fallen downwards. They might have been warned by the smell of burning, but since the same smell pervaded everything outside there had been no special distinction... Probably the fire was only small, a mere fuse box trouble, but to four beings only a sixteenth of an inch high it represented a roaring furnace.

"Outside!" the Amazon said abruptly. "This has ruined our plan for future breakdown, but our lives come first. If we stop here we'll fry—and quick."

She levered herself up quickly to the ventilator grille and slipped through it to the broad metal base platform outside; then she helped Viona, Mexone, and Abna as they followed her. For a moment or two they stood looking about them, seeming to be on a kind of metallic rimrock with smoky void below and green-lit vacancy above.

"We'd better—" the Amazon started to say, then she broke off with a choking gasp as something descended over her head and dropped to her feet, imprisoning her. She had no chance to say anything for Abna, Viona, and Mexone whirled on top of her, likewise caught by the same object… And suddenly the bag, or whatever it was, sailed outwards into space, through smoke and green light.

"We're in a net!" Abna panted, trying to struggle to his feet amidst ropy strands. "Caught like four damned butterflies—but who's responsible I can't tell as yet. It looks as though we're being carried somewhere."

His guess was right. By the time the four had sorted themselves out and verified the fact that they were indeed in the toils of some kind of net, it had been placed on what appeared to be a plain—either the floor or else a table. Imprisoned in the folds, furious at their capture, they stood waiting—but not for long. Gradually they realized that the laboratory was taking normal form, was no longer a wilderness of gigantic pillars and misty distances.

"We're being enlarged to normal size again," Viona

gasped abruptly.

"Looks like it." The Amazon gave a grim look at the netting, which with every moment was becoming tighter. Soon it burst entirely to shreds as the four continued to increase in size. Something else was also visible now; the gradually appearing figure of Lixom himself, arms folded, watching the enlargement process in grim calmness. And beside the instrument for controlling the enlargement stood one technician, watching intently. At his feet were the remains of an object like a butterfly net.

In the distance there was hazy confusion, smoke, and a good deal of activity as technicians fled to and fro. Then, finally, the growth enlargement ceased. The four found themselves back at their natural stature. Lixom still surveyed them from his gigantic height, cold detachment in his dark eyes.

"Frankly," he said finally, when he had dismissed the attendant technician, "I am not impressed by your conduct after I had given you every facility to do as you wish. You will recall that I warned you not to do anything foolish."

The four did not respond. They stood waiting, racking their brains to decide what move to make next.

"It is fortunate," Lixom resumed, "that I kept track of your various activities with television. I had a presentiment that you would try something reckless, and I was not disappointed. The only trouble is you acted so swiftly I had hardly time to grasp your intentions before they were accomplished… I watched your tour of this laboratory, your attack on my controlling scientist, your size reduction, and finally the mishap to one of the time-controlling machines. I had lost track of you due to your smallness but I guessed the truth. To find you and net you was not difficult... Fortunately, the damage is not too grave. But obviously we cannot have you amongst us, as we had hoped. You are not to be trusted."

"All right, let's end the pretence," the Amazon snapped. "You are intelligent enough to realize that in our position you would do the same. You would not stand idly by and see your universe gradually destroyed if you could do anything to stop it."

"I would if I knew the odds against me were too heavy. You don't seem capable of realizing that. This outburst of yours has shown that, on every occasion, you will do what you can to upset our very necessary experiments."

"Certainly we will," the Amazon said, glancing at the grim face of Abna beside her. "Nobody else in the universe except us knows what is happening, or going to happen, and we're willing to sell our lives to stop you. You consider it a scientific experiment, a necessity to your universe. We regard it as cold-blooded annihilation over a period of years."

"And whilst you are about it," Lixom said, "what would you call the fate of my controller, hurled into past time without the least warning? That, Amazon, was murder!"

"It was necessity," she retorted, her eyes glinting. "It

was fighting you with your own weapons."

"Does it occur to you that the controller would meet his death? Sent into a past time he would finally resolve in space itself at a point before this vessel filled that space. He would die instantly in the airless void."

"It was necessary," the Amazon said stubbornly. "I make no apology for what I did."

Lixom sighed. "All this is very unfortunate. I had hoped we could cooperate with our different sciences: now I see that that is impossible. It would perhaps be fitting that you suffer the same fate as the controller, then I shall not have it on my conscience that I put you to death. I have a dislike of the barbarous; sending you into a past time where you can no longer cause trouble is much more pleasant, don't you think?"

The four did not answer. In fact there was nothing they could say, but each one of them flinched a little inwardly as they realized what was implied. Flung into a past Time, which inevitably would mean they would materialize in space somewhere in the past, was worse than any death-sentence.

"So it shall be then," Lixom said, after a moment's pause. "And it shall be done now before you can do more damage. Walk down that aisle-way."

The four turned and obeyed. Each one of them hesitated for a moment over their proton guns, then failed to use then. Even if they could perhaps annihilate Lixom their liberty would only be brief... There were too many technicians about to make escape feasible. And in any case, escape to where? They were aboard a mighty, hostile spaceship, and after what they had done nobody was their friend. Further, Lixom now had a weapon in his hand as he came up behind then. Evidently he was fully prepared for any attack upon himself.

Striving desperately to think of a way out of the situation the four kept on walking, but they were not directed towards the Time-controlling machine they had fused, but to an instrument unlike any they had ever seen before. It was, as usual, of huge dimensions and infinite complication.

"Stop!" Lixom commanded abruptly; then he moved forward a little to face the four. "This is a duplicate of the Time device in the control room," he explained. "You will remember that I sent your Ultra into a past time and presumably it is still traveling—in Time, not in space. Things will be swifter for you because you represent less mass than the Ultra, therefore your flight backwards into past Time will be infinitely faster. I offer my condolences to all of you... You will simply occupy the space outside which existed before this space ship came into this universe. You will not actually move in space at all."

Lixom did not say any more. Turning to the machine beside him he snapped a bewildering series of buttons. To the four standing together within its range there was a sense of immediate annihilation. They felt certain they were going to die as nameless forces crashed in on their senses. All feeling, vision, and hearing vanished and they were paralyzed entities in some unknown region between Here and There.

They stumbled and reeled over into darkness, convinced that this was the end and that they had found a resting place in the eternal void somewhere back in the Past...

CHAPTER 4

THE DYING WORLD

It seemed strange to the Amazon, lying in a huddled heap with her eyes closed, that she should be able to think. Yet why not? Could death destroy the power of thought? She had often wondered about that and arrived at the conclusion that thought cannot be destroyed, and goes on forever.

She was thinking—and clearly, which was an interesting point. She didn't feel any pains, either, nor did she feel the biting unimaginable zero of outer space. It was cool, certainly, even bitter, but to compare it with the absolute zero of the void was absurd. And yet Lixom had distinctly said—

Slowly the Amazon opened her eyes. She lay trying to weigh up the view. For some reason she was in weak sunlight, not the darkness of space. Because she was lying on her side the view was horizontal instead of vertical. There was a sort of scrubby plain half down her line of vision, and the other half comprised a weary-looking pale blue sky.

Sky? Sky! Suddenly she sat erect, amazed. She

wasn't in space at all, but on a world of some kind, perhaps about the size of Mars to judge from the horizon distance. Her eyes traveled quickly from blue sky and sandy, scrub-ridden desert to Abna, Viona, and Mexone, all of them sprawled in various postures in the dust. In another moment she had hurried to them and began to revive them. They too, like her, gazed about them in astonishment as they got slowly to their feet.

"But this is incredible," Abna said at last. "It savors to me of a miracle. By all normal standards we ought to be dead in the void, yet—"

"There's only one answer that I can see," the Amazon said. "Somewhere in the past a planet must have existed in exactly the same spot as the Lixom's spaceship now occupies. When we were hurled backwards into Time, how far we don't know, we automatically came to that planet instead of landing in space. I'm sure that's the answer," she went on, looking about her. "This is a dying world, as is evidenced by the thinness of the air; and it's practically a waterless one too to judge from the dust and sand and the few cacti-like plants."

"It would seem," Abna said slowly, "that Lixom hurled us back tens of thousands and even millions of years."

"Could be." The Amazon gave a nod. "It doesn't matter much, and we can't estimate it without instruments. The fact remains that we're here, and not much better off than before." She glanced quickly at the sun under her shaded hands. "Mmm, a dwarf star of some kind, and with the reddish yellow tinge of a star already on the wane. At the time of Lixom's spaceship that star must have been completely dead—burned out. We never saw it anyway, and we haven't actually moved much in space itself, only in time."

"Somehow," Viona commented, "this looks rather like Mars. Do you suppose there are any people?"

The Amazon shrugged. "How should I know?"

They were all silent again for a moment, gazing around the endless desert. In the distance, stirred by a sudden windstorm, a great cloud of reddish dust climbed into the sky. Otherwise there was no movement, only a sense of infinite quiet and utter desolation.

"The position," the Amazon said grimly, "is a tough one—tougher than any we've yet had to face. Lixom is carrying on with his universal destruction, and we're separated from him by the barrier of numberless centuries. For once we can't get at him. We might if we had the Ultra with its Time-controlling device, but even that's gone too."

As the Amazon had said, the position was a tough one, but even so they had been granted the miracle of life when they had expected death. There might yet be other miracles in store.

"I suppose," Mexone said, looking at Abna, "you can't exert your metaphysical powers to the full, Abna, and get us out of this?"

Abna laughed shortly. "Impossible, I'm afraid. There are limits even to what I can do. I couldn't possibly master Time and space to such an extent—and even if

I did what avail would it be? To arrive back on Lixom's spaceship certainly wouldn't be to our advantage…" He braced himself and looked over the desert, "No, we've just ourselves to rely on—and the Power that made us in the first place. At least we've got weapons if we have to defend ourselves. We'd better look around for food and drink, as the first essential."

They began walking, quite aimlessly, since it didn't particularly matter where they went. The air retained its thin coldness and would probably have occasioned extreme discomfort had they been normal beings. As it was, possessed of superhuman strength and accustomed to atmospheric peculiarities, they continued moving without distress.

"This world is certainly nearing the finish," the Amazon remarked, as they progressed. "That sun hasn't moved a fraction in all the time we've been here. Presumably there is eternal daylight here. Since it's only rarely that a planet has one face to the sun, we are forced to the second assumption. Namely that this world is so old that tidal drag has finally slowed its revolution completely and it is no longer turning. Like a top wound down, it has one face to the sun as it slowly peters out its life."

"Seems like it," Abna agreed. "The most alarming consequence of that, to my mind, is likely to be the absence of water. This desert seems to be as dry as a bone."

"There may be something beside the scrub plants," the Amazon said. "Some sort of liquid which they absorb to keep alive. We'd better look."

They pressed on until they came to an outcrop-ping of the cacti-like plants. Queer, drab yellow things they were, leathery, and armed with fine hairs, each of which had a yellow tip. Viona was on the point of reaching out to one of then to examine it when the Amazon snatched her arm back.

"Don't, Viona."

Viona looked surprised. "But I was only going to—"

"Touch the plant. I know. Those yellow tips look harmless enough hut they might be venomous. We're on a world about which we know precisely nothing, remember."

Viona relaxed, realizing there was a good deal of truth in what the Amazon said. Then she turned actively to work as, with large screwdrivers for "trowels" they began to dig into the dry and dusty ground. Cracked, dry clay fell away under their efforts, revealing the snaking roots of the cacti-plants. Lower still the clay vanished and gave place to soil of an earthly type.

Lower still, at a depth of about a foot, the soil had a slight dampness—and finally at three feet of depth, with the quartet flat on the ground and scooping away for dear life, there was actual water. The Amazon dipped her, finger in it and tested it on her tongue. She made a wry face.

"It's water all right, but pretty foul. Tastes as though it has come out of an oily radiator. Not that that will matter when we get really thirsty… As for food, that's another problem altogether."

She straightened up on the edge of the hole and sat looking speculatively at the cactus outcropping. The leaves with their leathery covering looked fat and inviting as though they might contain edible vegetable matter of some kind... Then in the midst of her appraisal, a shadow flitted suddenly across the sun, and distracted her. She looked up quickly and gave a start.

"What are they?" Viona demanded, who had seen the flying objects at the same moment. "Birds? Carrion crows?"

The Amazon did not answer. With the others she was staring skywards at about two-dozen strange objects hurtling through the sky, wheeling, and coming back again. They moved at a speed faster than any bird, yet they had no visible wings. In every sense of the word they were fantastic. Some were straight and thin, like eels; others looked like flying tridents; still others were just balls that expanded and contracted as they flew... And gradually they were coming nearer, and lower.

"I don't like the look of this," the Amazon said abruptly, getting to her feet. "They're hostile from the look of them."

She snatched out her proton gun and waited, feeling curiously defenseless in the emptiness of the desert. In a moment Abna was at her side, his own gun ready, and Viona and Mexone stayed on their knees, weapons at the ready, their eyes to the skies.

Then, suddenly, as if by telepathic command, the weird flying horrors descended, directly towards the Crusaders. They ducked the onslaught and fired their guns at the retreating "flock." Two of the eel-like ones dropped, but the others wheeled round and came back.

"Let 'em have it!" Abna snapped, and he pressed the switch of his proton-gun fiercely. He blasted one of the tridents out of the sky, but another of the eel-like creatures hurtled down and sent the Amazon spinning, her gun flying out of her hand.

Immediately she was in the grip of something that possessed incredible tenacity. It was like a flying leech, and equipped with tremendously powerful suckers. They clamped on the Amazon's bare throat and she immediately felt a horrible, dragging sensation as the vile object sought to draw blood from her neck through her skin.

She was only at a loss for the moment, taken by surprise. And in that moment she realized Abna, Viona, and Mexone had their hands too full protecting themselves to come to her aid—so she went into action on her own account. She clamped her steel-strong hands round the leathery dryness of the thing's body and scissored her legs upwards to catch, its tail-end between her knees. It lashed and struggled savagely, but it could not break free; nor did it let go its hold on the Amazon's jugular, which seemed to be its main point of interest.

Straining mightily with her arms the Amazon forced her strength forward inch by inch, the muscles rolling on her shoulders and her face a mask of blind, savage strain. Harder and harder she forced her arms upwards, her grip on the thing's body never relaxing—

then suddenly her right knee slipped and the thing's tail lashed free.

From then on it was like a small and incredibly ferocious snake doing its utmost to win victory. Still hanging on to force the thing from her neck the Amazon lashed and rolled in the dust. The others glanced at her, still firing at the things as they hurtled down from the skies, but they had no chance to help her without leaving themselves open to attack...

Sand poured into the Amazon's mouth and eyes, into her ears, as she rolled over and over, tearing with superhuman power at the deadly thing determined to draw the life-blood out of her. In a whirlwind of dust and sand the interlocked two rolled within the region of the huge cacti-bush. Again the Amazon tried to lock the thing's tail between her knees, and again she failed. She realized with a frantic desperation that her strength was not proving equal to the task. Blood and energy were both being drawn from her by this fantastic leech, and she was becoming unequal to the struggle.

She essayed a final effort to tear the thing from her knee. The struggle sent her rolling low down into the cactus bush. She felt her senses reeling, her arms becoming slack—but oddly enough the "leech" was no longer fastened to her. It lay upon her fallen body but its suckers had left her neck. Panting, exhausted, she tried to imagine why. She screwed her head round and looked at the others. Viona and Mexone were still firing their guns as fast as they could, decimating the creatures in mid-air—but Abna was engaged in a struggle similar to the Amazon's. One of the trident-shaped creatures had fastened on to the great vein of his thigh, and he was engaged at the moment in striving to tear the trident apart with his bare hands—a half bent, massively muscled figure against the dusty background of the desert. Then the Amazon's senses left her.

She returned to consciousness with the bitter after-taste of restorative in her mouth. She stirred and looked about her, conscious of a returning strength after the appalling weakness she had formerly experienced. Abna was squatting looking at her rather ruefully. Behind him, sprawled on the ground, evidently recovering their strength, were Viona and Mexone.

"It's not often I do that," the Amazon said, struggling to a sitting position. "That horrible creature took all the life out of me, even if it did mysteriously cease its activities half way."

"Good job it did," Abna said. "It provided us with a weapon. Take a look."

He nodded to a point nearby. The Amazon gazed at the eel-like object with which she had struggled, then as she gazed more fully she noticed perhaps half a dozen yellow-coated hairs projecting from it. Mere wisps, and barely visible.

"Cactus hairs?" she asked.

"Exactly—and your early guess that they might be venomous is proved correct. In your battle with that atrocity you rolled into the bush. Fortunately you were low down out of reach of the leaves, but that thing was on top of you and brushed against the hair-tips. That was when it died. I've had a look at it, and as far as I understand its complicated setup it suffered an immediate and total paralysis. Evidently it is a provision of Nature for the plants to protect themselves."

"Evidently." The Amazon fingered her throbbing, red-whealed throat and looked at the empty sky. "Where have they gone?"

"Scared off. I defeated one of the trident-things that was doing its best to finish me, and dashed over to you. When I saw the dead one with cactus hairs on its back I guessed the truth. I snapped off one of the leaves, taking care not to touch the hairs, and held it in readiness for further attacks by the horrors. Believe it or not there weren't any! The moment I held that leaf up they just vanished. Evidently they know by some sort of instinct that the plant is deadly."

The Amazon got to her feet slowly, still holding her aching throat. Abna looked at it critically.

"Nothing to worry about," he said quietly. "It's badly marked where that thing fastened itself on, but otherwise you're unhurt. The restorative will make up for the blood you've lost."

Abna patted the restorative flask in his belt and then looked about him.

"Viona and Mexone are all right," he added, as the Amazon glanced towards them. "Just resting up a bit after the battle."

"Nice life they have on this world," the Amazon

commented bitterly. "Hardly the kind with which to cooperate and exchange ideas."

"Hardly. Yet it's Just the kind of life one ought to expect on this world, cone to think of it."

"You've analyzed it, then?" the Amazon asked quickly. "For myself I'm at a loss. It seemed to be partly bird, partly animal, and partly reptile."

"None of those things, Vi. The answer is—bacteria."

"Bacteria!"

"Exactly. Fungi, unicellular, and rod-shaped. Born of decomposed organic bodies and grown to abnormal size from the smallness one usually associates with bacteria."

"Yes, I believe you're right." The Amazon stood thinking for a moment. "It is generally admitted by science that bacteria, of human size, will be the last form of life to present itself, born of the bodies of dead animals and humans that have gone before. The toughest, hardest type of life known: just the type to endure the rigors of a dying world. Life that can stand fantastic extremes of heat and cold, shaped in rods, bars, and balls… Yes, you're right."

"I think so," Abna nodded. "And the greatest foe of the bacteria is this type of plant with its swift venom… What the giant bacterial life feeds on I don't know— or even if it feeds at all—but human life and blood certainly seems to have an unholy fascination for it. That form of life is something we've got to be wary of henceforth."

"Obviously." The Amazon stretched her arms and

eased her legs up and down gently. "Well, for myself I feel about recovered again, so we'd better carry on from where we were attacked. We were in the midst of digging for water. What do you suggest we do? Collect some of it in our pack-bottles?"

Abna nodded. "Could do. We're going to need it sooner or later so we may as well grab it now we've dug for it." He signaled Viona and Mexone. The two came over, and for the next fifteen minutes they spent their time slowly filling the empty water bottles, which they always carried with them.

The liquid showed muddy brown as they collected it—not at all intriguing hut it might, at a pinch, keep life going when they got desperate.

"And finally, food," the Amazon said, fixing her bottle on her belt slot. "What do we do about that? I'm commencing to feel hungry even as it is."

"I can think of only one thing—those cactus plants." And as the Amazon looked at him with misgiving Abna added, "Yes, I know: the hairs with their yellow tops are poison, but that doesn't say the plant itself is. Come to think of it, earthly nettles sting dreadfully, but the leaves can be eaten or form the basis of a beer without any harmful effects. The same thing might apply here."

"And how do you propose to find out?"

Abna shrugged. "Only one way."

With that he unfastened a knife from his belt, and then unclipped a small pair of tweezers. With the help of both he cut off one of the leaves, pulled off the deadly hairs, and then looked at the leaf as it lay in his palm—thick, fat, and somehow inviting-looking.

"It's worth a try," he said. "If I've guessed wrong I can save myself by metaphysical power before poison takes too strong a grip."

With that he broke off part of the leaf and chewed it slowly.

The taste was not unpleasant, rather like solid port wine, if such a thing could be imagined. The Amazon, Viona, and Mexone stood watching, plain anxiety in their faces.

"It seems to be—" Abna started to say; then suddenly he gave a gasp. He tried to move but only dropped to his knees as sudden unimaginably violent pain smote him. It felt as though a solid bar of white-hot iron were reaching from his throat to his stomach, paralyzing every nerve. He dropped gasping to the sand, spewing the remains of the leaf from his mouth. He was conscious of the Amazon's hands clawing at him desperately.

"Abna! Abna, what do I do? Tell me!"

He fought frantically for words. "No-nothing. Leave me to fight...fight this thing. I'll... I'll beat it." He turned over on his face and beat the sand with his fists, striving against the anguish that was devouring him. Somehow he secured the necessary mental detachment to fight against the virulent poison convulsing him, a poison so vicious that his skin turned a bright salmon pink in every exposed portion where the venom flowed through him.

Horrified, helpless, the Amazon, Viona, and Mexone stood watching him, powerless observers of a mental fight against death in a few seconds. They saw his body quivering with the force of his mental efforts; they watched his fists pounding uselessly into the sand to mitigate the torture he was enduring... Then gradually, very gradually indeed, these convulsive efforts began to cease. The salmon pink of his skin assumed its natural mahogany-brown. Quietly he relaxed into the sand and lay breathing hard and stormily.

"Are you...better?" the Amazon ventured, stooping beside him.

He moved slowly and turned over to look at her. Finally he gave a wry smile and struggled into a sitting position.

"Better now, yes. I can understand now why the bacterial life has no love for this stuff. It's more than poison: it's like an atomic explosion in every nerve and organ. I'm afraid that's one form of food we won't be having."

"And apparently there isn't any other," the Amazon said. "So what do we do?"

"I don't know," Abna said quietly. "I just don't know."

There was silence for a moment; then the Amazon sank down beside him into a sitting position. Viona and Mexone squatted nearby, waiting for any suggestions that might come forth.

"Of course," the Amazon said presently, "we don't know for certain that this world is devoid of intelligent life which might be able to help us—give us food and shelter. A stranger from another world landing in Earth's Sahara Desert might easily assume that Earth was deserted."

"True, but he would at least have a spaceship with which to tour the planet and find out the truth," Abna pointed out. "Further, if he'd seen bacteria flying about he'd know that life of an intelligent understandable type had vanished... We haven't got a spaceship with which to tour. We haven't got *anything*, not even food."

"Yet on the other hand we can't just sit down to the situation and admit we're beaten," the Amazon protested. "That's quite unthinkable."

"Yes, but... At least let us be realistic, Vi. On other occasions there has always been a way out some-where—but this time there isn't a thing. The cupboard's bare at last. No ship ever again, no food, only bacterial life eager to destroy us... And if we start walking in order to try and find a race of people, if one even exists, we can't keep up the tramp for ever. I'm afraid we've been granted the miracle of life—in the shape of this planet when we expected death—only to find that death has caught up with us after all."

"Well, I refuse to accept such an idea!" Viona exclaimed. "And I'm surprised at you, dad, for offering it. It's so utterly unlike you with the powers you've got... Maybe the hangover of that poison is producing a depressive effect on your mind."

Abna frowned for a moment. It was clear that such a thought had never occurred to him. There was even the possibility that it might be true.

"There must be a way of some kind!" Viona insisted, scrambling to her feet. "Why don't we walk and try and find it? If we die walking we'll have at least tried."

"She's right," the Amazon said, as Abna glanced at her. "We can't take it lying down, Abna. We've never done it yet and we're not going to do it now."

With that she got up, and Abna did likewise. He gave a wry smile as he saw Viona's youthful form marching ahead, full of the determination to do something even if she didn't know what.

A few yards behind her tramped Mexone, not quite sure whether it was a sensible idea to walk until extinction caught up…

Then suddenly there was something different, just as the Amazon and Abna were preparing to follow Viona. They both saw the saw phenomenon at the same moment—some curious mirage forming in the desert, by no means an unusual occurrence in a waste space like this.

Evidently Viona had also seen the mirage forming, for she came to a sudden halt and stared ahead. The vision was not more than a few feet distant from her.

"Do you see what it is?" the Amazon gasped, as Abna gripped her arm and stared intently. "That's no ordinary mirage! It's a spaceshtp of some kind—"

The phantom vision took on deeper detail, like a photograph coming into view under the influence of developer.

"It's the Ultra!" Abna shouted hoarsely, as for a few seconds the monster shape hovering just clear of the desert sands took on solidity, to almost as quickly start fading again. But in those few seconds, things happened at lightning speed, things that were entirely in the hands of the active Viona, the nearest person to the phenomenon.

The moment she recognized the Ultra she didn't waste precious seconds absorbing the impossible. Instead she raced forward with all her energy, the sand flying under her shoes. In just the brief tine in which the Ultra assumed definite outlines she reached its airlock and seized hold of the projections—then to those watching in the desert she became misty and disappeared along with the ship, as though neither had ever been… There was a swirl of disturbed atmosphere, and nothing more.

"Viona!" the Amazon shrieked, horrified. "Viona!"

She made to hurl herself forward towards the spot where the girl and the ship had disappeared, but Abna restrained her.

Mexone came running back, utter amazement on his face. "What happened?" he demanded.

"Plenty of things," Abna told him. "Not a miracle, but a scientific possibility, which let us hope will save us in the finish. It's up to Viona now, and she never was anybody's fool."

"But— Where's she gone?" the Amazon cried. "How did the Ultra get here like that?"

"I'm surprised the answer hasn't occurred to you," Abna responded. "It's this question of Time once again. The Ultra, journeying through space and time on the trip on which Lixom sent it, has finally caught up with the same few moments of Time where we are. It's evidently still going further back into Time whereas our backwards Time movement has ceased here. Fortunately it was clear of this planet by a few feet otherwise I don't know what would have happened—a violent explosion I imagine, as two bodies tried to occupy the same space and Time at the sane moment..."

"But..." The Amazon made a bewildered movement, her usually keen scientific intelligence disturbed by the disappearance of Viona. "How can the Ultra have caught up with us when it was sent into Time so much ahead of us?"

"It was sent at a slower speed than us. Don't you remember Lixom saying he could hardly afford the power to send the Ultra into Time; and don't you remember him saying later that we four would be a far easier proposition than the Ultra? It's come through Time more slowly than us, and finally caught up and continued on its way."

"With Viona hanging onto it!" the Amazon exclaimed. "What do you suppose will happen to her?"

"I don't know." Abna's voice sobered. "She'll take care of herself if she can, and she isn't without ingenuity. Just have to trust to luck..."

The Amazon became quiet, her eyes scanning the desert anxiously. Under any normal circumstance, no matter how outlandish, she would have remained calm—but this time there was a difference. Viona was her daughter, and it was at times like this that the

Amazon became a worried, confused woman, and not the coldly scientific paragon she usually was. Abna too, though he didn't say much, was assessing the possibilities—and he just could not imagine what had happened to the girl now she had been snatched into both Time and space.

"There's one thing evident," Mexone said presently. "You are quite right in your reasoning about the Ultra catching up with us, Abna. That's proved by the distance away it was from us, which is almost the same as the distance to the outside of the giant spaceship from the control room. Spatial distances haven't altered much. There's only the Time-factor involved."

"Right enough," Abna agreed, "and as regards Viona there's one thing in her favor. The ship was just clear of the ground in the few seconds we saw it. Right?"

"Well?" the Amazon questioned.

"Well, as it moves backwards through Time it will presumably stay in that position, which means that Viona will have atmosphere as long as she's outside the ship. She won't be in void, or anything like that. Presumably this planet will be present for millions of years backwards, so—apart from topographical changes in the shape of mountains, which could rise and crush the Ultra in its backward flight, I don't think there's much danger."

"In any case," Mexone said, "Viona won't stay on the outside of the ship. She's bound to try and get inside it, a simple enough job if she can shift the external clamps…"

Which, at that moment, was precisely what Viona was trying to do. And her position was an extraordinary one, to say the least. The moment she had taken hold of the Ultra she became a part of the backward-Time movement embracing it, though she was not aware of the fact in her urgency.

She had definitely acted on the spur of the moment, to find herself in the midst of the weirdest changes whilst she hung on to the Ultra's projections. All about her was the desert, rising and falling curiously as, in the passage backwards through Time the formation of the desert changed slightly, rising or falling as sand accumulated or fell away. It was to Viona rather like watching a movie film in reverse, only the uncomfortable thing was that she was a part of it. One thing she did know: she was alone. Completely alone. Her mother, father, and Mexone had vanished into thin air—even as she had done to them—in the first few seconds. She was left hanging desperately to the Ultra's projections, conscious of the fact that if she let go she would drop into a Time somewhere in the past and the Ultra would continue on its way, to be lost forever.

After a brief look about her she began to straggle sideways along the Ultra's armored hull. Tenaciously hanging on, fighting the disturbed air currents that produced a strong wind about her, she edged her way slowly towards the airlock, wondering whether she would ever make the distance, clinging by mere toe and finger holds.

She called on every reserve of her great strength,

trying not to notice the chaotic changes going on about her as, with the passage backwards, the desert began to slowly change into soil, rivers magically appeared, and there was the ghostly suggestion of mighty ruins building up into vast, imposing edifices. Dimly she realized that she was coming to a time when a civilization had been on this planet.

Then she reached the airlock. Bracing herself she fumbled with and finally turned over the exterior clamps, which automatically unfastened the interior ones as well. She waited as the great metal barrier swung open, then with a thankful sigh floundered through the short passageway into the control-room. It was like coming hone again to be within the Ultra's huge and comfortable confines.

She snapped the switch which closed the airlock again, looked through the window at the vision of vast cities where the desert had formerly been—cities changing even as she watched in the swift flickering of night and day as the planet once more assumed a normal revolution; then she turned to the Ultra's own Time-controlling apparatus.

She was not at all sure of her ground as to how the position stood. As far as she knew Time-controlling forces had started the Ultra on its backward journey through Time from Lixom's spaceship, and once within that backward stream it would keep on going until jerked out of it by superior power. Lixom had said that the power that had started the Ultra off had not been of very great strength. Therefore—

Viona nodded to herself as these thoughts passed through her mind. She switched on the power plant, then gently eased in the Time-controlling settings. When nothing happened and her heart began to thud heavily with anxiety, she advanced the power a little more, the setting being on future-Time instead of past. This done, she looked worriedly through the window— and gradually, to her delight, she beheld that which she had hoped to see.

The backward-effect was slowly coming to a stop. The strange cities that hung like four-dimensional cubistic nightmares around the Ultra were no longer building to greater size as the past was penetrated. Instead they were coming to a halt, until finally after a long moment of pause they began to slowly dismantle themselves again, clear proof that the backward move-ment had been stopped and the Ultra was now moving future-ward.

Viona heaved a sigh of satisfaction, slightly increased the power, then set herself to watch intently through the observation window. She surveyed with fascinated interest the slow destruction of the cities amidst the flickering of night and day.

She saw the mighty creations of intelligent life end in rubble and change thereafter through swiftly moving centuries into sand.

She noticed the flickering of night and day becoming longer and longer as the planet's revolution slowed down—until at last there was only day and an appearing desert below.

Viona turned, reduced power, and then went back to the window.

She was coning back to the brief period where she had left the others on her astonishing dash into Time.

And at last she saw them, only for a moment, in the desert, then they were gone again. Quickly she stopped the power and reversed the Time-gear. Backwards, ever so gently, a fraction at a time until at last three well-beloved figures merged phantom-like out of thin air, frantically waving their arms and racing forward through the sand.

Viona reached out to the switches and snapped them out of contact. Freed of all influences the vast vessel thudded down to the waste of sand and became still.

CHAPTER 5

STALEMATE

The Amazon was the first to reach the ponderous airlock as it slowly opened. She hurried straight through to the control room and imprisoned the grinning Viona in a bear-like hug.

"Thank heaven!" the Amazon whispered, kissing her. "Thank heaven! I've never been so scared in all my life as when you took a flying leap into Time."

"I told you, she'd be all right," Abna, smiled, coming in. "Nice work, Viona—and congratulations on split-second thinking. If you hadn't have done that the Ultra would have sailed on forever, out of our reach."

Mexone came forward and gave Viona a hug, then he looked at the Amazon rather critically.

"Your mother's rather in danger of becoming a woman,'" he said dryly. "Whilst you were gone I saw a woman for the first time. The Golden Amazon was simply nowhere."

The Amazon gave Viona a final affectionate pat on the shoulder and then straightened up.

"All that's over now," she said briefly. "I regret the

display of silly emotionalism, but I just couldn't help it: that's one of the faults of being human and not a pure, dispassionate scientist." She crossed to the switchboard, actuated the lever that closed the airlock, then said, "We'd better have a decent meal and decide over it what we're going to do next."

Viona nodded and with Mexone headed towards the provision stores. Abna watched her go and gave a whimsical smile, then he glanced towards the Amazon.

"In an emergency, Vi, she's obviously to be relied upon."

The Amazon shrugged. "Of course. Look who's daughter she is. Oh, I include you in the credit," she added, as Abna began to vaguely protest.

"Thanks. I'm glad to hear it… Anyway, all else apart we've got everything back as we want it. Thanks to, Viona. So what do we do next? Forget all about Lixom and his crazy schemes or go back and tackle him?"

The Amazon did not answer immediately. She was too busy thinking the problem, out; but when the meal was underway she essayed an answer.

"You speak rather loosely, Abna, of forgetting all about Lixom… We obviously can't do that. For one thing we owe it to our consciences to defeat his designs, and for another we'd have nothing to go to in a few years if the Universe is destroyed."

"We could go backwards in Time to a period where Lixom has never been heard of," Viona commented. "That way we could luxuriate and enjoy ourselves…" She wrinkled her nose. "But somehow that doesn't appeal to me."

"I should think it doesn't!" the Amazon said coldly. "What do you think we're the Cosmic Crusaders for? No; we can't leave things undone like this. We've got to return to the battle. We're entirely justified in doing so because Lixom has not a single conceivable right to be in our Universe—even less has he a right to destroy it in order to correct an imperfection in his own experiments."

"All right—we're agreed we fight him," Abna said, eating hungrily. "What moves do we make? Don't forget he'll know we're there the moment we appear near his ship, and if he gets the better of us a second time it'll be the finish. He'll make sure of that."

"I was thinking of the Zero-Thought Amplifier as a matter of fact. He won't be able to argue with it. His ship, and everybody inside it, will be reduced to nothing in a few seconds. Provided of course we can get to within range without him being aware of us."

"The Zero Amplifier has limited range," Viona said. "At a distance near enough to be effective we'll probably be detectable..."

"For myself, I don't altogether like the idea," Abna said, surprisingly. "It's too ruthless. We have to defeat Lixom's purpose, I agree, but to suddenly destroy him and his scientists is not in keeping with the Cosmic Crusaders. Remember, he has what he thinks is a perfectly just reason for doing what he is doing, and that lives have to be snuffed out in the process is to him nothing more than the killing of insects. Remember how he mentioned that fact?"

"I remember it," the Amazon conceded grimly. "I also remember that he hurled four scientists— ourselves—into time without a single compunction."

"Two wrongs don't make a right," Abna shrugged. "I still say we've no call to behave like barbarians just because he did so on that occasion. We also hurled one scientist into Time and death. At least we presume he died. Remember the foreman?"

The Amazon made an irritated movement. "Look here, Abna, if we're going to go about the universe like a bunch of saints, refusing to take any violent action, we might as well quit right now. It can't be done. Surprise and destroy the enemy: that's always been my principle. In an emergency we'll never get anywhere without those methods."

Abna spread his hands. "All right—but let's to ourselves be true, at least. If we are going to destroy Lixom and his merry men, let us give him warning first."

"Yes, it would be a pity if we weren't polite about it," the Amazon retorted acidly; and for a moment there was an uncomfortable silence, at least so far as Viona and Mdxone were concerned. Abna himself was not in the least perturbed. The outlook of himself and the Amazon was always at variance: she believed in direct action and no questions asked, whereas he took a more tolerant view. Usually the Amazon found herself forced to accept Abna's outlook, but not without first discharging her feelings as she had on this occasion.

Finally, as the meal finished, the Amazon roused herself to comment.

"Very well, Abna, we'll do it your way, and tell Lixom first what we plan to do. We'll give him a deadline to be on his way, and if that isn't obeyed we'll act promptly. Agreed?"

"Agreed," Abna said quietly.

"But," the Amazon added, "if he shows the slightest sign of being nasty—as I've every reason to think he will—I reserve the right to release the Thought Amplifier upon him instantly, and control it myself."

"As you will," Abna shrugged. "All I'm trying to do is avoid having too much on our conscience."

"With the Universe at stake that's a pretty poor excuse," the Amazon commented. "One doesn't argue with something deadly. One kills it, instantly..." She got to her feet and crossed to the switchboard. "We'd better be on our way then."

She started up the power plant, then studied the Time controls and noted exactly the position in Time in which the Ultra stood.

By the readings she would know, when eventually Lixom was contacted again, just how many years or centuries intervened. Without comment, she eased in the power on the forward Time-control and stood gazing through the window, grim-faced and not at all pleased with the situation. She felt that she had the opportunity for instant and complete annihilation of the enemy, and to pass it up by a conciliatory approach went definitely against the grain of her character.

Moodily silent, as Viona and Mexone cleared away the remains of the meal, she stood gazing through the window on the slow changes taking place in the desert. Abna came over and joined her in silent watching. As year gave place to year, and in time to centuries—during which the Ultra did not actually move in space at all, but only in Time—the desert slowly passed away into one enormous glacier; and presently, at one period, the sun flared brilliantly for a brief spell and then died down to a mere glimmer, which ultimately passed away into darkness. And, outside, the glacier landscape reflected icy stars so clear and sharp that it was plain there was no longer an atmosphere present.

"So that's what happened," Abna murmured, arousing himself. "The sun of this world turned into a nova, and then became extinct, leaving this world as a frozen hulk in the cosmos. It must at some point break up and leave the space which is later to be occupied by Lixom and his spaceship."

Such indeed proved to be the case. In a couple of centuries more the glacier world fractured—but it was not a natural occurrence. Out of space there came a gleaming point, which rapidly grew to a flaming ball, sweeping ever nearer the Ultra and the world on which it stood. Abna and the Amazon stared at the advancing, blazing enormity from the heavens with utter wonder.

"It's a small runaway star," Abna said finally. "They do happen occasionally, but it can't hurt us since we're moving through Time quite rapidly and are only in one spot for about a three-millionth of a second. The chance of that thing striking us at the exact moment is too big a coincidence to worry about."

He was right. They were conscious of the runaway star arriving and shattering the glacier world, creating vast cracks in its surface, but they themselves were not affected. They continued their journey through Time on a cracked and crumbling world, whilst the runaway star slowly receded into the remote depths of space.

Then finally the glacier world collapsed entirely, already badly fissured and broken by its collision with the runaway star. When that happened the Ultra was adrift in space, motionless in regard to it, but still moving rapidly through Time into the future. The glacier world became cosmic dust in the void and was as though it had never been.

Years and centuries still passed on, and Abna and the Amazon gazed in thrall at the marvel of their trip. Never in all their experiences had they made so long, or so interesting a journey through Time only. And beside them, equally fascinated, sat Viona and Mexone, watching the eternal shift of the distant stars as hundreds of years fled by.

So it went on, for countless centuries that were nevertheless being accurately recorded on the instruments—until abruptly they realized they were faced with something that looked like a gigantic wedge of darkness blotting out the stars.

"It's Lixom's vessel!" Abna exclaimed, but even as he spoke the Amazon had grasped the truth and dived for the switchboard, instantly cutting out the Time-control before the Ultra actually resettled against the giant spaceship's side. As it was the Ultra halted its weird advance and stood motionless in space and time, the mighty spaceship of the colossi people at a distance of several miles from them.

"Well, we're back," the Amazon said, looking at the instruments. "And we've covered a time of...twenty seven thousand centuries. Or, two-million, seven hundred thousand years."

"Interesting," Abna commented. "And now we face fresh problems in making contact with Lixom."

The Amazon looked at him surprise. "Why do we?"

"Well—consider," Abna insisted. "We are now at a point in time before we ever contacted Lixom. He and his people don't even know we exist at this stage. We're up against the paradox that always comes with Time-journeying. If you ask how do I know that we're in a Time before our advent I'd reply that the Ultra proves it. We're free in space, not attached to the side of the giant spaceship, as we would be if the Time were later. If we were later still we'd be moving into the past, hurled there by Lixom's Time-controlling apparatus. I know it all sounds terribly complicated, but Time is always that way. At the moment we are before our former arrival, but since as we know there are countless alternative paths through Time we are not compelled to do exactly as we did before. We have taken another route and can live Time twice over in a different way. Whether or not it applies to inorganic things like the Ultra I don't know. Probably it does."

"It sort of fits in," Viona mused. "At this Time before, the Ultra was in space. It's in space again now, and for all we know to the contrary it is exactly the same space as before."

"Exactly," Abna agreed. He thought for a moment, struggling to sort out the complexities, then he said, "If we drift into the same Time wherein we had our earlier experiences, Vi, we don't know what may happen. We may he at the mercy of the Ultra's movements; we may even dissolve. I can't work it out. So our biggest safety lies in going some considerable distance beyond the Time when we were hurled into the past. That way, we'll have a clear field of Time."

"How about four years ahead of our former experiences on this giant vessel? Four years ahead of the time when we were flung into past time?"

"That should be safe enough," Abna agreed. "It's a period of Time in which we have never been, so we'll be able to proceed normally."

"But how do I calculate it?" The Amazon looked in puzzlement at the instruments. "I just don't know where to begin."

"There's an easier way than involving yourself in a mass of complicated four-dimensional math," Viona said. "Set the Ultra advancing into Time again and go to a point where this big spaceship has disappeared. Then work backwards a little way in Time. The result will be that you'll be well ahead of the period of our first visitation."

"Yes, but…" The Amazon stopped and thought, then

she shook her blonde head. "Clever reasoning, Viona, but there's a snag, and a big one."

"And it is?" Abna questioned.

"Well, if we advance to a point to where the big ship isn't in existence any more we're bound to cross the time where the Ultra was hurled into the past by Lixom. What's going to happen then?"

"Mmm," Abna said. "One would think the infinite calculus mere child's play compared to the Time problem— Wait a minute! There's a way out of that, too. Go into advanced Tine via hyperspace. Make a detour as it were. That will cut out normal space and Time altogether for the period of the operation, and we'll resolve again into normal space at a point which we think should be clear of the big spaceship."

"Which leads us to something else," Mexone, who had been making notes, remarked, and the Amazon glanced at him.

"What?" she asked.

"Lixom gave five years as his tine for the universe dissolution to take place. We propose going ahead a good deal further than that and working our way backwards. What happens if there is no Universe to resolve into? In plain words, where are we if Lixom succeeds in his efforts?"

"He won't! He hasn't got to!" The Amazon clenched her yellow fist and beat it gently on the shelf of the switch panel. "In any case, moving forward will give us an idea what's happened—or what is going to happen. I'm prepared to risk there being no universe when we resolve again, if the rest of you are?"

"Go ahead," Abna said, and turned to once more gaze through the window, with Viona, and Mexone on either side of him.

There was a pause as the Amazon, aided by the central computer, made the necessary computations for the hyper-spatial Time-trip, then she closed the appropriate switches and threw in the master control. Instantly the Ultra seemed to drop into bottomless nothing—a sensation to which the four were accustomed from previous journeys through hyperspace.

Outside, the stars whirled and vanished into utter darkness.

Inside, varicolored lights and displays winked in tune with the controls and power plant. The whole thing was automatic and flawless, devised by master-scientists. And the master-scientists themselves steeled their nerves and organs against the ghastly sensation of endless falling, a sensation similar to being in an elevator hurtling at high speed down a bottomless shaft.

Then suddenly a click. Controls operated themselves; the rhythm of the power-plant changed slightly. For the Crusaders the sensation of bottomless falling ceased so suddenly that they stumbled. They caught hold of the window ledge and stared outside.

There was the Universe, just as it had always been, and showing no sign of harm. It swept into limitless distance in a haze of stars, nebulae, and cosmic dust.

"So much for Lixom," the Amazon said, with a grim

smile. "We are now approximately fifty years ahead of his Time and the Universe is quite intact, so it's obvious he doesn't succeed in his plans to destroy it. Why that should be so we don't know as yet."

"Since we know the answer there's no reason for us to go on risking our necks," Mexone commented.

"Yes there is," the Amazon told him. "We may be the reason that the Universe is intact. If that is so Time will force us into action, no matter what we do. Anyway, having seen things this far we're certainly not retreating."

"You said fifty years ahead of Lixom's advent?" Abna asked.

"Exactly fifty," the Amazon said, looking at the readings. "Which of course we've by-passed so we didn't see what happened during those years. Our task now is to work backwards slowly until Lixom's space-ship comes into sight. Then, just a little bit further back until we can act."

She turned to the switchboard and then hesitated, looking out onto space. A frown crossed her face.

"That's odd! Where did that planet come from, I wonder?"

The others looked, and gradually discerned what was apparent to her. At a comparatively near distance there was a dark world—yet it reflected the starlight. It had certainly not been there before, and planets are not in the habit of suddenly appearing in the short space of fifty years.

"Very strange," Abna said, pondering. "I confess I

don't understand it. It's reflecting the starlight pretty strongly which seems to suggest it's sheathed in ice... Don't ask me how it got there."

They were all silent for a moment trying to fathom the mystery. When finally no solution presented itself the Amazon gave a shrug.

"Beyond me. We'd better start moving back and give Lixom the shock of his life."

Her hands went to the Time-controls and in one blur of movement—as far as the exterior was concerned—the fifty years were instantly hurdled. Oddly enough, nothing was changed. The unexplained planet was still there. The four looked at it, then again the Amazon shifted the controls, more delicately this time as a shorter period of Time was demanded. In jumps and spurts, leaving the exterior a confused unintelligible jumble each time, the Ultra hopped back down the years until at last there was something understandable. There was Lixom's vast spaceship, and all traces of the mystery planet had disappeared.

"Here we are," the Amazon commented, looking at the instruments. "As far as I can estimate—and it's only an approximation—we are about eighteen months ahead of the Time when Lixom hurled us into backward Time. In other words, eighteen months have gone by since he got rid of us."

"And from the look of things, I can well believe it," Abna said, peering through the window intently. "There are distinct evidences already of his activities. Take a look."

The Amazon joined him, and so did Viona and Mexone. They stood gazing out onto the further reaches of the void, and to their eyes—accustomed as they were to scanning the cosmic deeps—there were distinct signs of blanks in the remoter seas of stars. In all directions, at the furthest limits, there were colossal areas of darkness, which could only mean one thing. Slowly but surely—having made enormous progress in the intervening eighteen months—Lixom's experiment was succeeding.

"And yet," Abna said finally, as he caught the thought in the minds of the others, "the ultimate answer is that the Universe is normal, and nothing can gainsay that. It's what happens to bring that about that concerns us. You'd better give Lixom his warning, Vi, by radio."

She nodded slowly. "I suppose I had, and the moment he knows we're back in his sphere of influence there'll be plenty of fun and games. We'd better be prepared for anything, and all of you had better stand by our weapons in readiness for trouble—except the Zero-Thought Amplifier. I'm reserving that for myself."

She waited whilst Abna, Viona, and Mexone each settled themselves on the seats before the Ultra's armory, each of them controlling respectively a giant proton-gun; an atomic dissembler; and a heat-ray. Usually these weapons proved sufficient for anything that tried to attack, but this time there was a doubt about it owing to the brilliant quality of Lixom's science, and his mastery of dimensions.

"Are we ready?" the Amazon asked presently, and

as Abna nodded she switched on the radio equipment, gazing meanwhile at the vast spaceship floating in the void some fifteen miles away.

"Calling Lixom of Dra," the Amazon intoned. "Calling Lixom of Dra. Come in please."

There was a long interval and then a too-carefully-enunciated voice responded.

"Radio operator responding. Who wishes to speak with Lixom? Where are you and what are you?"

"The Golden Amazon speaks," the Amazon replied coldly. "I must communicate with Lixom immediately..."

There was silence, and probably a good deal of consternation at the other end—then at last the grave, unhurried voice of Lixom responded. Evidently the radio operator and he had taken time out to fit their little voice transformers before answering.

"This is a surprise, Golden Amazon! Though why it should he I can't imagine. I have had a respect for your scientific powers even since we first met, which was why I sought to be rid of you. It would appear that I was not successful... My scientists tell me that you are a few miles away in the Ultra. Even more remarkable! Presumably you recovered it."

"Obviously. And I wish to tell you, Lixom, that—"

The scientist cut in again. "I know exactly what happened to you, Amazon. You, and those with you, fell upon a dead world that used to occupy the space where this spaceship now is. Then presumably your Ultra caught up with you in the Time-channel. Yes, my controller told me of that possibility."

The Amazon gave a start and glanced in amazement at Abna, Viona, and Mexone as they gazed towards the speaker.

"You remember the controller you so efficiently hurled into Time, surely?" Lixom gave that slow, rumbling laugh. "He too dropped into the Time-channel which deposited him, on the world that once was here, only it seems that he merged into that world much further back than you, at a time when that world had a vast and progressive civilization, and its scientists a very good knowledge of Time-travel. When he explained his predicament they returned him through Time to the spaceship. He told me it was quite possible that a similar experience would befall you four. So you see, though I am not quite conversant with the details, I am not altogether surprised that you survived and came back."

"At least," the Amazon said, "I am gratified to know that the Controller was not killed: that relieves my conscience considerably. I suppose he didn't tell the advanced civilization he contacted what your real purpose is?"

"Why should he? It could hardly concern that civilization since they are in a past Time."

"Such a civilization existed all right," Viona murmured. "I saw it for myself..."

The Amazon glanced at her, nodded, then spoke again.

"I am communicating with you, Lixom, to issue a

warning. For myself I would never have considered such a course, but the others insist on it because you are a scientist striving for a certain objective—the contraction of our Universe-molecule. As inhabitants of that molecule we protest against your ruthlessness—and if I had my way you'd be blotted out without warning. However, that is not in keeping with a policy we adopted long ago when we became the Cosmic Crusaders. We resolved then that we would keep to the right as far as possible, and that's what we're doing now. You are given a warning, Lixom, that if you don't instantly stop your activities and depart to your own universe we'll destroy you completely and utterly."

"With your Zero-Thought Amplifier, I suppose?"

"Exactly." The Amazon frowned at his uncanny awareness of her intentions. "How did you know?"

"Merely a matter of deduction. You have no other instrument in your scientific armory powerful enough to annihilate us. And our answer is a simple and direct one—the warning will not be heeded. I have already explained what we are doing, that this molecule-universe must be eliminated to bring perfection to our own science. Everything must be sacrificed for scientific progress, and that includes your type of life. I regret it, but progress is a hard master..."

"You will find us harder," the Amazon retorted.

"That remains to be seen. I don't fear you or any of the instruments you can bring against us. From here on we shall proceed with our work and ignore you... Yes, I said ignore you. I know we could bring you here again quite easily, but it would demand too much trouble to keep you constantly under observation. Thank your gods that you have escaped death so far, and when finally this molecule-universe shows signs of complete dissolution—as it will—you can still preserve your lives if you wish by returning into a Time before any of this happened. Those are my final words to you, Golden Amazon."

There was a click, and then silence. The Amazon looked at the radio equipment, her violet eyes hard and bright with a barely controlled fury.

"He's insufferable!" she declared finally. "A brilliant, egotistical, overbearing—"

"For some reason," Abna said, grinning, "I rather like him. I always did. Oh, I know all about his scheme of annihilation, but once again I say he isn't doing it from that aspect. I don't think he even considers it. He's got to eliminate a molecule, and he's going to do it regardless. Only once did he get really annoyed, and that was when we bust up some of his equipment. Then he tried to be rid of us, not by cold-blooded murder but by sending us into Time. I'd wager he probably even guessed—or perhaps knew with the equipment he's got—that we'd land on a world. After that it was up to us."

"What are you doing? Holding a brief for him?" the Amazon demanded angrily.

"Heavens, no—but you've got to admit he's not in the usual run of power-drunk scientists, such as we've come across many times in our travels. Consider things now. He's not going to bother with us any more: he'll get on with his experiments and be damned to us."

"No he won't!" The Amazon swung, her mouth a vicious, tight line, to the Zero Thought Amplifier. "Principles or otherwise, Abna, we're still inhabitants of this Universe and it's up to us to save ourselves and everybody else. We know things will be saved in the end, and I don't see who else is going to do it but us. I'm going to use the Amplifier," she finished, adjusting the controls on the small boxlike device.

Abna did not say anything: he knew it wouldn't be much use, anyway. The Amazon was determined to follow what she believed was the right line of action, and in such a mood nothing would stop her. Silent, Abna watched, Viona and Mexone beside him.

The necessary adjustments did not take the Amazon very long. Then she sighted the boxlike instrument towards the enormous, distant spaceship and switched on the power at the highest notch. Simultaneously she concentrated, and watched eagerly.

By all the laws of science the spaceship should have dissolved instantly, every scrap of its material make-up reduced to zero by the law of thought being higher than the law of materiality. So it had been on past occasions…but not this time. The ship remained where it was, untouched, and the Amazon stared in utter wonder. Then finally she stopped concentrating and switched off.

"It's incredible!" she whispered. "It isn't operating."

She was about to say something more then stopped

as the radio warning light blinked suddenly. She switched on and leaned over the microphone.

"Well?" she demanded. "Golden Amazon speaking."

"I said I had had my final words with you, Amazon, but maybe I should have a few more so that you can correct an illusion with which you seem to be laboring. I shouldn't waste time using the Thought Amplifier on us. Thought, remember, assumes different forms and ratios in different universes. Whilst I agree your Amplifier must be superb in dealing with anything in this Universe, which is your own, it is hopelessly out of tune with something from another universe, like ourselves. Do you think for one moment I would have ignored an instrument like that, which I studied when I examined the Ultra, if it could have been of any use to us? Hardly! Forget your plans to destroy us, Golden Amazon. Clever though you are there is nothing you can do!"

"We haven't finished yet, Lixom," the Amazon snapped.

"No? What an amazing amount of energy you waste on a useless proposition. Rather silly for such highly intelligent people, isn't it? Well, if you must flog yourselves to death, there is nothing I can do about it."

Again the click, and then silence. The Amazon stood with her lips compressed, heating her yellow fist gently on top of the radio equipment. Abna cocked am amused eye towards her.

"If you and Lixom each had a sword you'd make grand team in a sparring match," he commented.

"Each longing to get the better of the other and neither of you succeeding... And he's right about one thing, you know. Thought does assume different ratios in different universes. That's one of the main premises in advanced metaphysics."

"Then why couldn't you have told me?" the Amazon demanded. "You let me go through all that effort and use all that power to no purpose!"

"I could have been wrong," Abna shrugged.

"And he knew I made the attempt," the Amazon went on, musing. "I wonder how?"

"Considering the quality of their science I wouldn't say there's anything peculiar about that. Probably have instdyruments on us that detect the slightest thing. The Amplifier would generate an appreciable electronic wave even if it didn't have any effect as far as thought is concerned. The wave would register on instruments."

The Amazon meditated through an interval, then finally she gave a sigh.

"I don't often—if ever—have to admit I'm beaten," she said, "but I confess I am this time. With our strongest weapon no use I don't know what move to make. And yet to leave things as they are, with Lixom having the upper hand, is obviously impossible. So," she looked at the others each in turn, "what do we do?"

CHAPTER 6

FOUR-DIMENSIONAL WORLD

There was a long silence in the Ultra. In fact the Amazon's confession had come as rather a shock. Usually in complete command of any situation it was something new to hear her admitting defeat. Yet, upon reflection, it was clear that was correct. The powers of Lixom were superior to her own.

"I can think of one possibility," Viona said presently. "Only I don't know, mother, if you'll disposed to adopt it."

"Tell me what it is, then I can soon decide."

"Why not go back in Time to the planet we found and contact their civilization? It was a highly orga- nized one from what I saw of it, and obviously they understand science or they couldn't have sent back Lixom's controller like they did. Enlist their aid and their science since, for once, we've bitten off more than we can chew."

The Amazon pondered, the expression of her face clearly showing that she didn't particularly like the idea.

"There's no other way," Abna said calmly, having thought out the details. "You're not exactly admitting defeat, Vi; you're going to enlist the aid of scientists who may have more advanced knowledge. Nothing wrong with it."

"That depends on how you look at it," the Amazon retorted. I have never yet in all my life relied on anybody else for assistance, and I don't like doing it now. But I'm afraid I've got to if I'm to get rid of Lixom. All right—we'll go."

She turned to the switch panel and surveyed the instruments, then she turned.

"We'll go forward in Time, turn into hyperspace, and then move through Time for twenty seven thousand centuries. In that way we'll once again detour round the Time where Lixom hurled us into the past."

"Check," Abna said, and with Viona and Mexone he began to prepare himself for what he knew was going to be an unpleasant session.

As indeed it was. Once again the Ultra faded into Time-space, moving ahead in Time to a point where that mysterious planet was again in evidence and Lixom's spaceship nowhere to be seen. The Amazon did not trouble to brood over the enigma, but continued straight on with her purpose. She set the Time-controls for the required 27,000 centuries backward Time-travel, then once more the plunge into Time and hyperspace and the conviction of everlasting falling.

It was becoming unendurable when at last it abruptly ceased.

The Ultra was motionless and around it loomed the desolate emptiness of desert that they had formerly seen.

"So far, so good," the Amazon said, disconnecting the hyperspace controls. "It's now a simple retrogression backwards until we come to the era of the cities you saw, Viona. How far back would they be, do you think?"

"I've not the least idea. I was too confused and worried at that time to think straight. I know they grew and grew and finally formed into sort of cubes piled on top of each other."

The Amazon frowned. "Cubes?"

"That's what they looked like. It may have been the effect of the Time-traveling, but on the other hand they could have been four-dimensional solids, almost incomprehensible to our three-dimensional senses."

"Interesting," the Amazon reflected. "We'd better have a look."

She set the Time-controls again and switched them on. Very slowly the Ultra began to move backwards down the Time-channel, the desert outside not taking on any changes as yet. That only came gradually. The changing of the sand into soil, the appearance of rivers widening swiftly. Foliage and vegetation springing up from decay into life. The ruins of cities building themselves out of the dust into giant structures, which, in turn, assumed the curious square effect that Viona had seen—and over it all the winking sunlight as it fled between night and day. So finally to the apparent zenith of building where the cities hung curiously remote and unexplained against a blue sky. At this point the Amazon cut the power.

With a jerk the Ultra became still in its Time-traveling and in silent wonder the four Crusaders looked outside. They had certainly come into the midst of a civilization, but of what type was it? That was what baffled them.

The Ultra was standing on mossy grass in the midst of a broad park-like space where trees stood at attention in the hot sunshine. Curious trees. One sort of saw them, and yet didn't. It seemed silly, but the four could not be sure they were looking at the trees. Their flat, not round, branches seemed to abruptly shear off into mist and uncertainty. The tips of the grass-blades round the Ultra did the same—and as for the massive building at the back of the park— Here indeed was something out of the wildest dream.

The building, in common with the others banked in serried rows behind it, was fantastic in the extreme. It was a kind of cube within a cube, like a small box inside a larger one. And there were no doors or windows visible. Nor, as the four continued to gaze in wonder on the scene, could they distinguish any streets or approach ways. The buildings seemed to have been dumped down in the park spaces and thereafter rose in fabulous terraces to the blue sky.

Nowhere a living soul, a sign of communication, traffic ways, or aircraft. Only these boxes within boxes that had no means of entrance or exit. And again there hung about them that odd lack of certainty; the impression that they were projected, rather than real.

"Well, we've seen some queer places,'" Abna said at length, rubbing his blond head, "but this beats the lot of them. Any ideas, Vi?"

"On the face of it I would say it's a world of four dimensions, populated by people who understand the fourth dimension as easily as we understand three or as a worm understands two. Scientifically, on such a world, we might not see an opening that is really there. It looks like a solid wall, but from a four-dimensional aspect it is actually open… Maybe I'm talking through my ear," she finished, shrugging. "We can at least look. I can understand Lixom's controller comprehending this lot because he's experienced in dimensional science, but it's going to be a tough one for us, I'm afraid."

Fully determined, nonetheless, to investigate they loaded themselves with provisions and water, checked their weapons, then stepped outside the Ultra, locking it on the outside. In the sunlight they stood and surveyed again the weird-looking trees, the "Alice in Wonderland" buildings, and listened particularly to the heavy, cloying silence that hung over everything. Finally it was Viona who made a comment.

"If this is a four dimensional world, why didn't it look that way further on in Time? The desert and scrub seemed natural enough. There wasn't the elusive quality there is here."

"In the future there is no civilization," Abna pointed out. "I think it is the civilization which is causing the effect since no world, in the ordinary course of events, would be four-dimensional in a three-dimensional universe. We'll find the answer in the kind of science these people have, I imagine. Are we ready to explore?"

"Entirely," the Amazon agreed. "Might as well try that box building in front of us and see what's in it."

They advanced towards it slowly, ready for the first sign of trouble, their hands resting on their proton-guns. But nothing disturbed the quiet, sunny stillness. Finally they reached the building and stood looking at it, and up at its immense height. It had a wall that seemed to a mixture of stone and metal, but certainly there was no way of getting in.

"This doesn't make sense," Abna said, irritated. "There must be some means of entrance. Let's try the back."

This they did, with no better result. Baffled, they wandered from building to building, through the whole huge terrace of them, but nowhere could they find a means of entry.

"It's ridiculous!" the Amazon declared flatly, staring at the buildings all around her. "Lixom's controller made contact with the people, so we ought to be able to."

"We can't get in, but perhaps they can get out," Mexone suggested. "How about doing something to attract their attention and see what happens? Tell you what, there's plenty of room in that park space. How would it be if I exploded a small bomb there? The din would surely be heard?"

"Try it," the Amazon nodded. "We certainly can't make anything of the present situation."

Mexone nodded and hurried off towards the distant Ultra. The Amazon relaxed against the curious metal-and-stone wall and glanced at Abna and Viona. They merely shrugged, completely at a loss as far as suggestions were concerned.

In the distance, Mexone finally reached the Ultra and disappeared inside. Presently he reappeared, clutching a small bomb to himself. He moved to what he evidently imagined was a safe distance, detached the safety pin, arid then ran for the shelter of the Ultra. The Amazon, Abna, and Viona turned their faces to the wall and covered their closed eyes—

The bomb exploded. Either there was something queer about the planet—apart from the fourth dimensional aspect—or else Mexone had used a larger-sized bomb than he had intended in his excitement… Whatever the cause it blew up with staggering violence, flinging the trio by the wall off their feet and producing a flash of such intensity that they saw it through their fingers and closed eyes. When at last they had possession of themselves again they were aware of a curling mushroom of radioactive smoke on the one hand and a great rent in the wall by their side. They had not intended any such damage, but since it had occurred there was no sense in not taking advantage of it. They waited until Mexone caught up with them and then the Amazon peered into the gap—to behold darkness beyond.

"Well, it doesn't seem to have brought anybody into view," Abna commented; then he looked at Mexone. "Was that one of the smallest bombs you used?"

He nodded. "It was, but I never expected an explosion like that. Yet," he reflected, "I suppose I should have done really."

"Why?" the Amazon asked, unhooking her atomic torch from her belt.

"This planet—or this area anyway—is four dimensional, therefore an explosion would be registered in four dimensions instead of three, causing greater sound, greater destruction, and a greater flash. I believe that's the answer."

"Could be," Abna agreed, rather surprised he had not thought of such a solution himself. "Anyway, it's cracked this building open so that's something worth having."

The Amazon switched on her torch and stepped into the gap of broken stone and metal. The brilliant ray before her seemed dim after the sunlight, and at first only shone vaguely into darkness; then as she advanced with the others behind her objects came gradually into view, objects which were stirring slowly as though aroused from sleep or unconsciousness. There seemed to be thousands on thousands of them, stretching back into every section of the strange box-within-a-box.

"Wait a minute!" Abna exclaimed suddenly, gripping the Amazon's arm. "Don't you see what they are?"

She paused, looking intently in the torch beam. Then she gave a sudden gasp. "They're bacteria!"

"Yes," Abna agreed grimly. "Thousands of them, arranged on sort of shelves. Either we've disturbed them, or else it's the fresh air coming in that's doing it—but they're the same savage brutes that attacked us earlier in our experiences. Later in Time than this, of course, when they're more developed—but these are definitely the prototypes."

The Amazon gazed on them again. They were all shapes, though smaller than when they had been encountered before. The eels, tridents, and balls were there—and so were countless other types. And they were all stirring, making a noise like dry leaves caught by a breeze.

"Look!" Viona said suddenly, pointing.

There was a fascination, and a horror, in the phenomenon she had seen. One of the eel-like shapes was lazily dividing into two, cleanly and neatly. In a matter of seconds the division was complete and two existed where there had been one. A "trident" did the same thing, even as the quartet glanced at it.

"We'd better get out of here," Abna said suddenly. "We've started something unpleasant breaking open this dome. The Ultra's a safer place to watch what happens."

The others did not hesitate. They stumbled out of that dank, dark place with creeping horror at their hearts. There was something indescribably terrifying about that queer leathery shapes spawning in the darkness.

"I don't understand it," the Amazon said, as they came out into the sunlight. "Those things can't be the inhabitants of this world. They're unintelligent and blindly ferocious. They can't possibly be the beings with whom Lixom's Controller communicated—"

"Look out!" Mexone gasped abruptly, and he deliberately shoved at the Amazon and knocked her to the ground. Twisting her face round she was just in time to see a couple of the trident things flying into the sunlight, wheeling, then coming back to investigate.

"We'd better move," the Amazon said, scrambling to her feet.

"I don't know exactly what we've stirred up around here but it certainly isn't pleasant. Let's go!"

She whipped up her proton gun and fired as one of the hurtling tridents came straight for her. It blew to pieces in mid-air, and the hiss of the gun beam sounded like someone twanging a taut steel wire, so oddly did sounds register on this peculiar planet.

Running at top speed the four rapidly covered the distance to the Ultra, and even as they did so the bacterial horrors came hurtling out of the fissured box-building, in twos and threes, then in half dozens, wheeling through the air at lightning speed and somehow scenting out the human beings who worked frantically on the locks of the Ultra. Only just in time did they release the exterior switches and blundered through the opening into the control room.

The Amazon rushed over to the control board and pulled the switch to re-close the airlock; then she looked through the window and gave a gasp of surprise. At an incredible speed the bacteria had multiplied, following the law of fission and dividing themselves to create their progeny. The result was that the air was now black with them as they still came in scores and hundreds from the depths of the shattered building.

"Well, what do we do?" Abna demanded. "We've stirred up a hornet's nest with a vengeance—"

"We'll blot them out," the Amazon decided. "It will be something of a joy to do that after the uneasy time they gave us. Get to your weapons, each one of you, and I'll fly over them. They're certainly not the beings we want to contact, and I imagine they're better extinct."

She waited until the others had seated themselves on the saddles in front of the Ultra's formidable armory, then she set the power plant in action. Slowly the huge vessel rose upwards until it was a hundred feet above the ground. Then it began to move slowly forward.

It was a most amazing thing, but the ground was hardly visible now. In all directions save for occasional patches, the bacteria life was spawning, multiplying, and flying in a million diverse shapes, blotting out the sunlight and causing the Ultra, to fly through a living fog of the things.

And the things themselves were creating plenty of trouble. They ejected deadly venom that streamed yellow down the observation glass; they blocked the exhaust fins until a blast from the power plant literally blew out their dead bodies; they crawled and flew over every part of the armored hull. For the dozens that were slain by the fast-operating guns and radiations, dozens more divided and came to the attack.

Quite unintentionally the four had released a whirling destruction—though even now they could fathom how it had happened, or what the creatures had been doing lying passive in their boxlike dormitory in the first place.

Back and forth the Ultra, flew, sprouting decimation in all directions. The Amazon caught glimpses of the exterior through the streams of venom on the glass and the gaps between the creatures. She saw the crazy box-like buildings as black protuberances in the midst of a likewise black sea. Everywhere the horrors were multiplying at a speed beyond imagination.

"We're never going to finish them at this rate," Abna said, glancing round from the sights of the proton-gun. "They're being born faster than they die—"

"All right, then there's only one answer." The Amazon locked the controls so that the Ultra, hung, helicopter-wise, stationary over the stirring blackness. Then she moved to the Zero-Thought Amplifier. "This ought to do it. The things are of this Universe so there oughtn't to be a failure as there was in Lixom's case."

She sighted the apparatus on the spawning desert of bacteria below, threw the switch, and concentrated. Instantly she cut the power down a little as thee terrible force of the instrument not only eliminated a circle of the bacteria below, but the ground beneath them, began to form into a bottomless crater.

Once she had the desired strength the Amazon went on with her task with cold efficiency. By the mere power of concentration, transmitted into the softly humming instrument as it slowly turned on its universal bearings, she eliminated the hordes far faster than they could multiply. It was as though a mighty razor were sweeping the stubble of creatures off the ground and buildings.

They simply ceased to be wherever the instrument cast its influence, and gradually the normal appearance of things returned—until in about fifteen minutes there was not a bacteria creature in sight. Air, ground, and box buildings were free again.

"Good," the Amazon murmured, switching the instrument off. "That would seem to take care of that. Now we'd better descend and decide what to do next. Frankly, I've no ideas about it. There doesn't seem to be anybody intelligent on the planet. I don't know if—"

She paused and gazed in surprise at the radio equipment. For some reason, its warning light was winking for attention. Instantly Abna crossed to the window and stared outside, but there was nothing visible—nothing, that is, to suggest a reason for the radio call.

Frowning, the Amazon switched on. She hesitated, unsure of herself, then said into the microphone: "Signal received. The Golden Amazon speaking. Who wishes to communicate?"

"Friends," answered a quiet, well-mellowed voice. "We wish to thank you for the wonderful thing you have done for us—and we wish to thank you personally. Marvel not that we understand your language and all about you: such things are but trifles to our knowledge. Only in one thing were we beaten—the problem of the bacteria-life, which you have destroyed. So in one thing at least you are greater than us… I repeat, we wish to thank you, in spite of difficulties."

"Difficulties?" the Amazon repeated.

"Precisely. You exist in three dimensions, but we exist in four. Therefore, we, and our creations are invisible to your senses, but you are not invisible to us. Sound, fortunately, operates freely in four dimensions, as it does in three, so you are able to hear us. Radio too can travel from the fourth dimension into three, so we have managed to communicate."

The Amazon glanced out of the window and saw only the blue of the sky. She asked a question.

"Whereabouts are you?"

"Below your Ultra, in a small city which you cannot see. You behold the empty landscape in front of the buildings when held the bacteria—the park-like spaces?"

"Yes, I see it," the Amazon assented.

"Our city lies there. The fringes of it touch the trees, which accounts in part for their odd appearance—their sheared-off foreshortened look. This planet in itself is not four-dimensional, Golden Amazon, but we as beings *are*, and so are all our creations. However, we would wish better contact with you than radio. May we have the honor of your company, and those with you?"

Abna, Viona, and Mexone nodded, their eyes wide in surprise. The voice of the unknown sounded genuine and friendly enough.

"We would be delighted to accept your hospitality,"

the Amazon answered, "but it will be difficult. How can we find you when you and your city are both invisible?"

"You are prepared to trust yourselves to our devices?"

"With reservations, yes," the Amazon answered doubtfully. "We have experienced a great deal of trickery in our experiences, and therefore we—"

"By all the gods we hold sacred, Amazon, no harm will befall you or those you love."

"All right," Abna said into the microphone, as the Amazon hesitated, "We'll do whatever you think best."

"Very well. Firstly, bring your Ultra down to the ground, secure it in whatever method you think best, then rely on our best efforts to assist you."

"Very well," the Amazon agreed, still with obvious wonder in her voice; and forthwith she crossed to the control panel and brought the great vessel down to the ground. Then she snapped the switch that opened the airlock and looked at Abna.

"Okay—carry on," he said, understanding her look. "I think that for once we've struck a people who are not hostile."

"Nevertheless," the Amazon said, examining her proton-gun briefly, "I've learned never to underestimate the enemy. How are the weapons on the rest of you?"

There was a quick check, everything was pronounced satisfactory; then the Amazon led the way through the airlock. Abna, shut and clamped it behind them, then they stood looking around on the silence from which they had "vanished" all trace of bacterial life.

"I wonder what happens now?" Viona asked, as moments passed and nothing happened. "Is this another trick on somebody's part?"

"I don't think so," Abna replied seriously. "I judged from that voice on the radio that we are dealing with a straightforward and very grateful person—"

"Look!" Mexone exclaimed abruptly. "By the trees there…"

The others gazed with him. The lowest branches of the queer trees were obviously being bent aside as something passed then, and presently there was the surprising vision, much nearer this time, of the dusty ground being churned up as invisible feet came nearer. There seemed to be four people, and their height— to judge by the stride—seemed in the region of six feet. They were also two-legged. All this the Amazon summed up for herself, then she started as a voice spoke quite close at hand. The same voice that had been on the radio.

"There is nothing to see, my friends, by your senses, but likewise there is nothing to fear. Just trust yourselves to us. I, Amazon, will assume the honor of directing you, and my three colleagues will take care of the others."

With that, the Amazon felt her upper arm taken in a firm but friendly grasp by a hand she could not see and she felt herself impelled gently forward. Glancing behind her she beheld Abna, Viona, and Mexone being similarly treated. There was nothing possessive or hurtful about the invisible being's grip; it was simply a guiding hand, and presently it led the Amazon into what seemed to her to be a clear area, until she hit against something she couldn't see. She rubbed her shin painfully and stopped. The area was apparently perfectly clear.

"My deepest regrets," apologized the voice. "I should have pulled you to one side. At the moment we are in my governing domain and just entering the room where I hold my audiences. There is quite a deal of furniture about which I should have warned you against... There, Amazon—feel around and you will detect a chair. Please be seated in it."

Feeling oddly foolish the Amazon did as bidden. It came as a surprise to her to find the outlines of what was definitely some kind of chair. She felt for the seat, and then, carefully sat in it. Slowly she relaxed and sat in it, giving the nearby Abna an indignant glance as he whimsically studied her.

"A classic example of no visible means of support," he commented dryly. "A few stage magicians back on Earth would give their souls for a secret like this!"

"I would remind you, honored friends, that it is not a secret," commented the invisible spokesman. "It is the outcome of necessity and the difference in your senses compared to ours. Actually, at the moment, you are in a large four-dimensional building, in the main room thereof. To you, none of this is visible. You are looking at the exterior and are able to see your ship a little distance off—and, to one side of it, the fractured domicile of the bacteria life. Correct?"

"Correct," the Amazon agreed; then she too gave one of her rare smiles as she saw Abna, Viona, and Mexone sitting awkwardly down in the emptiness and gradually relaxing.

"So it looks funny!" Abna commented, cocking an eye on her.

"It looks, and is," she confirmed.

"Now, honored friends, you have some measure of comfort," the voice resumed, "and I am seated with my colleagues, facing you. And that, I am afraid, is the best that can be done to bridge the gulf between our differing senses. Firstly, may I renew our gratitude to you, for what you have done in destroying the bacteria creatures. They were the biggest menace to our safety, and by destroying them you have brought us a measure of security unknown up to now."

"I'm afraid I don't quite understand," the Amazon said. "Surely you would be invisible to the bacteria creatures?"

"Invisible yes, but not undetectable. Those bacterial objects have a sixth sense intensely developed, the same kind of sense which many animals possess on your own far-off world. They know by instinct where an object is, and can strike at it. That was how it was with the bacterial creatures. Always we were threatened by them. They could strike at us and destroy us, viciously. Even the fact that we had subdued them for a time was only a temporary thing; we knew that one day they must break forth again and seek to wipe us out."

"Was there any particular reason for them wishing to destroy you?" Abna asked. "Outside of blind ferocity, I mean?"

"Perhaps they considered themselves justified," the voice said. "They are the rightful inhabitants of this world, and we are not. We have only sought asylum here before we travel to another planet to domicile ourselves completely. That planet is now under the process of modification with our machines."

"Modification?" the Amazon questioned.

"I will explain. Originally we came from a world that had been made four dimensional by our experiments. We left it due to certain hostile elements who objected to our experiments and we decided to stay temporarily on another planet until we got an entirely virgin planet converted to our way of living. This planet is our temporary stopping place, as I have said—and the planet to which we will finally go is one of the many in this region. An entirely empty world, which our machines are remodeling to suit our peculiar circumstances."

"Then," the Amazon said, "I would suggest that you do not delay your departure. In spite of our decimation of the bacteria beings they will return—in some measure at least—at a later date. We know that because we've been in future Time, at the near-death of this world, and have fought the bacteria."

"So some must have escaped to remote parts," the voice mused. "That being so they will multiply rapidly and again constitute a menace. About how far in the future, would you say?"

"I don't know exactly. Some thousands of years."

"Mmm. We shall be gone by then, but our thanks to you for the warning. You have at least destroyed the immediate threat, which gives us time to turn round and perfect our scientific tasks. We did what we could to achieve temporary security by erecting those buildings, all interconnected, which are a concession to three and four dimensions. They are gigantic traps, one opening into the other, and filled with chemical substances that we have found these bacterial beings love. Substances akin to those in the human body, as a matter of fact—carbohydrates, fats, proteins... However, once within these traps the creatures could not find the way out. Unwittingly they entered three-dimensionally, as was normal, but once beyond the imprisoning walls they were in four dimensions with no idea how to escape. And the bait being a stronger lure than our invisible selves, they sought it instead of us, which was just what we wanted them to do."

"Then why did you fear them, if they could never get out of their traps?" the Amazon questioned.

"We knew that finally the traps would be full, and once that happened the things would look elsewhere— and attack us, and of all the instruments we have we have none capable of destroying their enormous toughness. They can be stunned but not destroyed. Even a direct hit isn't completely effective because the part untouched breaks away and forms a new creature. So there was nothing we could do—until you came along. I do not wish to pry into your secrets, Amazon, but what did you do to so completely wipe them out?"

"I used the power of negative thought amplified a thousand-fold, the basis of the thought being the non-existence of matter. Since thought is of a higher order than materiality, it won the victory. The prevailing belief, that materiality in the shape of the bacteria, was non-existent came into being."

"A wonderful conception, honored friend, a conception higher than any we have conceived in our own science. You are to be congratulated."

"Not entirely," the Amazon said. "The invention is a product of another science, belonging to a far distant world. We know how to operate our Amplifier, but we are not at all sure how it works."

"Nevertheless it was amazingly effective, and our thanks go out to you. The bacterial life, incidentally, is I think born of the flesh and blood race who once populated this planet, but where they have gone I know not."

"A vicious form of life indeed," the Amazon sighed. "But it has its match in a later Time in the shape of vegetation which generates a poison so deadly that even the bacteria succumbs to it."

"So it must always be," the voice mused. "A greater power always arises to crush the lesser..." He broke off suddenly. "But I am a poor host, honored friends. May I not offer you refreshment? Although you will not see it, you will certainly taste it."

"We would be delighted," the Amazon responded gravely, and in the brief silence that followed she relaxed to ponder the utter fantasticality of the situation...

CHAPTER 7

DUEL WITH COLOSSUS

The refreshment was the most amazing business ever, an eating of food from plates which could be felt but not seen; and a drinking from likewise invisible glasses. Nevertheless the contents of each were delightful and stimulating, producing even a mild intoxication in the form of high spirits. Though she was always on top of her form, the Amazon reflected that she had never felt so good as she did now. Sheer well-being flowed through her every nerve.

"I am rather curious to know why you came here," the voice resumed at length. "We saw you arrive, of course, and waited to see what you would do. Your first move seemed to be towards the bacteria traps and it appeared to us as though you were trying to get inside them. Then one of you exploded some kind of bomb, and the main trap was partly demolished. Before we could examine the puzzling situation further the bacteria onslaught started... It was after it was over that we decided to communicate with you. Why *did* you come? What was your purpose?"

"We need help," the Amazon said simply.

"Help! You who have science high enough to travel in Time and space, who are clever enough to bend even thought to your own uses. You need help? That is hard to believe, honored friends."

"Maybe, but it is so. You too are past masters in science, yet the problem of the bacteria was beyond you, was it not? As we helped you there—though I admit we didn't know we were doing it at the time—so you can perhaps help us. In fact if your four dimensional planet is to escape annihilation in future Time you have got to give us all the knowledge you can."

"It is not quite clear what you mean, Amazon."

"Far in the future," the Amazon said, "there is a group of scientists who are bent on destroying the molecule which you and I know as our own universe. They are doing this for scientific reasons because the molecule—as it is to their Universe beyond this one— is causing an upset in their scientific experiments. For no other reason, I would add. Even so, that involves all planets, stars, and life in this universe. And although we know of the danger we can find no means of stopping it. The ship from which these scientists operate is impregnable, and even proof against our Zero-Thought Amplifier because thought in their universe is of a different order to ours."

"Yes, that would be so," the voice mused. "But why do you come to me? What made you think you could rely on us?"

"We don't know that we can. It happened that my

daughter here had glimpsed your cities and—" The Amazon stopped and gave a little start. "But she couldn't have done! Your cities are not visible."

"That is true," the voice agreed. "What you daughter saw were either the many bacteria traps we have, or else the civilizations from which the bacteria originally sprang. Not that it signifies. Please continue your story."

The Amazon shrugged. "I have told it. There is only one thing about which we can be hopeful: in our journeys into future Time we have seen the Universe to be normal, which proves beyond doubt that somehow these scientists are defeated. At the present moment I cannot think how, and a careful examination of Time en route hasn't revealed it, either."

"There is one thing my wife has neglected to mention," Abna remarked. "He felt you might help us because you understand dimensional science, and Time—as do these cosmic scientists we're talking about. One of them has already visited you., and you returned him to safety."

There was a little gasp of surprise. "Not the creature called Giu?"

"We don't know his name. We only know him as the Controller of Lixom's time equipment."

"But that is the man! He came into our Time a much shaken man and said he had been projected into Time by four people of another race— He must have meant you! He was an enormous creature, many times bigger than the biggest of you!"

"That's he," the Amazon said grimly. "One of the men from the supra-universe beyond ours. In our efforts to defeat them we projected him into a past time and we heard afterwards that he had come here."

"That is so. We cared for him until he had recovered from his shock. It is interesting that he could see us, which he put down to his knowledge of dimensional science in which he and his race are highly proficient... Yes, we returned him safely through Time to his spaceship, but he said nothing of the experiment to which you refer."

The Amazon laughed shortly. "He hardly would in case you tried to upset their arrangements..."

"This," the voice said thoughtfully, "requires quite a deal of thought. As I understand it, you are saying that the universe is threatened with extinction by these beings—which of course will in the future involve our world too; yet on the other hand your own study of the future has shown that the plan does not materialize. And you want suggestions as to how to destroy these people?"

"Not necessarily destroy them, but most certainly stop their activities. We have no wish to actually harm anybody, but obviously their depredations must not be allowed to continue."

"Neither must yours!" a cold, booming voice commented.

Completely startled, the Amazon jerked her head round. So did Viona, Mexone, and Abna. To their complete amazement they found themselves gazing at the gigantic figure of Lixom himself, not very far distant. As he became aware of scrutiny he came forward with enormous, majestic strides.

"I shall have to withdraw my statement that I would have no further words with you, Amazon," he said dryly. "Obviously necessity demands that I shall, and you and your comrades have created that necessity."

The Amazon said nothing. She was staring in blank amazement, trying to imagine how this unexpected turn had come about.

"I see you are puzzled," Lixom said calmly, coming to a halt. "A brief reading of your thoughts expresses profound astonishment that I should be here. But why not? If my controller can come into the past, surely I can? He did it because you made him: I have done it deliberately because I wished it."

"Why did you wish it?" Abna demanded.

"I felt it better to discover what you had in mind. When I relinquished apparent interest in you on your recent return to a position near my spaceship, it was only a personal relinquishment. Instruments watched you all the while, keeping a check on your movements. They revealed that you had departed into Time, and the reading indicated a Tine in which my controller had already been. That I found interesting: what could you want here? I decided to come and find out for myself—and from what I have heard in the last few minutes I consider it a good job that I did. I gather you are planning our elimination?"

"Naturally!" the Amazon snapped. "And we'll never

stop planning until you leave this universe alone and return to your own."

Lixom turned, surveying apparent emptiness with his big dark eyes.

"And you hope for assistance from this person?" Then with a gesture he continued, "I can see him clearly, even as did my controller, thanks to my dimensional abilities. I behold a small, old-looking man, Amazon, and three others grouped about him— all of them gathered together in a single great room. Intellectuals, beyond a doubt, with no physical powers whatever. And these are the beings whom you think might prove our masters?"

"They have as much reason to wish to be rid of you as we have," the Amazon retorted.

"Maybe so, but it is not our intention to depart until we have concluded our task. I have made that clear often enough." Lixom hesitated for a moment, as though making up his mind about something, then he said, "I have tried all along to avoid the necessity for violence, Amazon, but in the end you have forced me to it. I cannot any longer tolerate these constant inter- ruptions in our work—interruptions fostered always by you and your colleagues. I have decided to oblit- erate you—and this other potential source of trouble in the shape of these four-dimensional people. There can't be any other answer."

There was the sudden sound of movement nearby. Lixom swung instantly, a weapon leaping into his hand. The noise of movement ceased.

"I would warn you against anything like that, my friend," he snapped, obviously addressing the four-dimensional being. "I can strike far quicker than you so don't attempt anything."

The Amazon eased herself in her invisible chair, putting her feet firmly on the ground. The one thing she realized at the moment was that Lixom's enormous back was to her as he turned to address the invisible host. Of course, he was gigantic in size, but then the Amazon had infinite faith in her strength and agility.

She gave Abna a meaning look as she poised herself, then suddenly she leapt with all the tremendous power of her leg muscles.

Like a living projectile she collided with the giant just as he was turning again, and the tremendous impact of her rush set him staggering for a moment.

Then indeed he realized why the Golden Amazon had got her name. This was no woman that was attacking him; it was a savage animal equipped with talons and muscles of steel. His weapon went flying instantly and a rain of blows descended on his face—blows which jolted and jarred his unaccustomed flesh.

He made a wild swing with his huge arms to defend himself, then he tripped backwards over Abna's deliberately outflung leg. Down he went, the Amazon astride his chest and her yellow fingers crushing into his great throat. Abna, Viona, and Mexone were also in action now, milling round the fallen, struggling giant like Lilliputians round Gulliver. One thing was proven now: in spite of his great size Lixom was of not particularly strong physique: at least in comparison to the steel-muscled Crusaders. At the end of three minutes hectic struggle he was flat on his back, gasping, his legs and arms pinned down and the Amazon holding his throat. She still sat astride his great chest as though riding a horse.

"You, Lixom, are an intellectual—and so are we in the normal course of events," the Amazon panted, "but at times it seems that muscular prowess is more rewarding."

"What do you hope to gain by this—this animalistic display?" Lixom panted, his great eyes blazing at her in fury.

"I'm not quite sure yet, but it does seem to me that you are better incapacitated than wandering about loose. You have deadly designs on all of us here, but only you can put those designs into practice. You can't get far if you're incapacitated, can you?"

"So you mean to kill me? Won't that be rather against your…principles? Those principles of which you seem so ridiculously proud?"

"We haven't killed you yet, and that isn't my intention either. You'll see what I'm driving at in a moment. Meanwhile we intend to make you secure…" The Amazon glanced up. "Mexone, there's nylon rope in the Ultra—several coils of it. Get it."

Mexone nodded and streaked off at a run. Abna promptly put on an arm to pin down the leg that Mexone had been holding. For a moment or two Lixom struggled again, then he gave up the unequal struggle and became passive. It was not long before Mexone was back and within ten minutes the giant scientist was so securely trussed from head to foot that he could hardly move. To haul him to his feet was something like trying to erect a telegraph pole. He stood swaying, trying to keep his feet, as the Crusaders smiled triumphantly at him.

"What do you intend to do, Amazon?" came the voice of the four-dimensional host. "Rarely have I witnessed such feats of strength as you four have just demonstrated—but I do not understand the reason for it."

"Nor I!" Lixom snapped. "This is sheer savagery— the sport of cavemen!"

"Maybe, but this time the sport of cavemen may pay off a dividend," the Amazon said dryly. "The main thing was to get you trussed up so you couldn't do anything. Now I'll tell you what we're going to do."

She picked up Lixom's gun, examined it then thrust it in her belt. After a moment she went on,

"You're coming with us, Lixom, back to the Time where your spaceship stands—or rather forward to the Time since it's in the future. You are going to radio your people to depart to their own universe because you have discovered an unexpected danger on your trip here... Naturally, the Ultra will be seen, but your answer to that one will be that you found the Ultra in this Time and used it to return to your ship. And, with the kind of compulsion we'll use, you'll most certainly give the message exactly as we want it."

"My people won't believe me!" Lixom snapped. "They'll suspect it is a trick and will destroy the Ultra and everything it contains."

"Including you? I hardly think so. They wouldn't dare risk destroying their leader." The Amazon shrugged. "Anyway, it's worth a try."

For a moment a thought crossed her mind—or rather a memory. Future time had shown the Universe to be untouched, which was the effect she hoped to achieve with her latest strategy—but it had also shown an unknown planet where Lixom's spaceship had been. Just where did that fit in? She shook her head to herself. It was one of the enigmas that might explain itself in the most unexpected way. The thing now was to further things as far as she understood them, and leave the rest to the dictates of Providence.

Turning, she looked at the area where she assumed her four-dimensional host to be.

"It would seem, my friend—or is it friends?—that this would terminate our visit. We came for help and instead have adopted something of our own initiative. But at least we didn't come in vain since we've saved you from the bacteria and—"

"Would it be possible for me to come with you?" the voice asked. "Though you assume you have the mastery—as you have at the moment—I am not at all sanguine of the future. I would rather see with my own eyes what happens."

"Join us if you wish," the Amazon smiled. "You are entirely welcome—and we'll return you to this Time when our task is ended." She turned to Lixom and slackened the rope slightly about his feet. "Start walking, Lixom—to the Ultra." He glared, then with shambling steps obeyed. Slowly the distance to the Ultra was covered and he was half lifted and half shoved into the control room. The Amazon waited until she was sure the invisible four-dimensioned scientist was safely inside then she operated the switch that controlled the airlock.

"Sit down, you," she said curtly, and gave Lixom a push. He reeled helplessly and thudded down on one of the wall bunks.

"Before we go," Abna said, crossing to the instrument panel, "there's something we can do to improve matters for our four-dimensional host—at least whilst he's with us. When he returns we can restore him again because he is accustomed to life that way."

"Meaning what?" The Amazon frowned.

"This." Abna moved one of the switches and set the master computer in action. He set a series of numbers and mathematical formulae, waited for the machine to figure out the result, then noted the answer. He grinned and nodded to himself.

"What are you doing?" the Amazon asked curiously. "We're wasting time."

"I've just been calculating the necessary figures to make our host three-dimensional instead of four whilst we are here together. The computer says it can be done, so here goes."

"Can't it be done as we journey?" the Amazon asked.

"I don't like wasting a moment if we can help it."

"Carry on," Abna assented. "I'll be a little time fixing up the equipment, anyway."

The Amazon switched on the power plant and set in the Time-shift. Gradually the vision outside began to change and smear amazingly as the forward motion through Time commenced. Lixom watched it all, interested because he was a scientist, but he made no comment.

Abna meanwhile was busy with a projector. It was a spare one, used for all kinds of conversions—heat rays, welding, cosmic patterning, and so forth—but this time it had a special purpose, or would have when he had finished his intricate alteration of its interior. Abna worked on steadily, to the fixed formula in his mind that had been shown by the computer calculations to be perfectly feasible...

The Amazon looked at him once or twice but did not question his actions. Outside, Time slipped by and the sun came and went with intermittent daylight... Lixom was silent, pulling at his bonds occasionally as cramp sought to deaden his limbs. Mexone and Viona remained near him, guardians in case he attempted anything.

Then at last Abna had finished his task. He straightened up from the projector, gave a final check to its interior, and then nodded.

"Everything in order," he said. "Now, my four-dimensional friend, where are you?"

"Here," answered a voice near the observation

window. "I have been watching you work, friend Abna—and very clever work it has been."

"Let's hope it works all right. I am assuming that you have no objection to being made three-dimensional, and visible, at least during the time we are together? It will greatly simplify things for both of us."

"I have no objections at all, providing I am restored when I return to my own Time."

"You have my promise on that. Now, this will be quite painless. Will you kindly stand there..." And Abna indicated a position in front of the projector. "Tell me when you have done it."

There was a momentary pause, then: "I have done that, Abna."

Abna nodded and switched the apparatus on. A pale yellow beam sprang from it, to the accompaniment of a soft humming note. The Amazon, Viona, and Mexone watched intently, and Lixom too seemed to be absorbed by the scientific demonstration taking place... And presently there were results. A phantom of a man in a toga-like tunic appeared—a mere ghost. Then he rapidly took on depth and detail and finally stood as the finished figure, a balding intellectual with an old, kindly face and wisdom in his eyes. Perhaps he stood five foot six. In every way he was similar to an Earthman in general physique.

"Good," Abna commented, studying him. "My reasoning was justified. At least it has made us able to see you, my friend, even though it will have limited several of your senses."

"Yes, that's true enough." The intellectual shrugged. "No matter. I am content to be three dimensional for the time being and leave other matters in your very capable hands… By the way, my name is Miastron. I don't think I have mentioned it so far."

"No you haven't," Abna agreed, switching off the apparatus and pushing it on one side. "Greetings all over again, Miastron."

The intellectual smiled and glanced towards Lixom. He met a cold, uncompromising stare in return. Abashed, the slender scientist looked away. The Amazon gave a grim look and went over to him.

"Lixom is going to pay for that little bit of incivility, my friend," she said quietly. "It won't be very long before he answers for quite a few things." She glanced at the instruments. "We have not a very great distance to go."

Miastron said nothing. He looked out of the observation window on the kaleidoscope of advancing Time, and in particular did he study the transformation of the sun into a nova and the final break-up of his temporary world before the onslaught of a wandering star.

"So that is how our haven ends," he murmured. "I have often wondered about it but never made the exertion to look for myself. Most interesting."

The Amazon went back to the switchboard, then after a long interval she said: "Prepare yourself, Miastron, for a rather unpleasant experience. For the purposes of Time-advancement we have to veer off into hyperspace, with most uncomfortable effect. However, there is no danger... You ready, Abna, Viona, Mexone?"

They nodded and prepared themselves. Lixom gave a puzzled glance, a vain stirring in his ropes, and then relaxed again. The Amazon fingered the switches that controlled the hyperspatial equipment and snapped them on. Immediately there was a sense of crazy reeling, followed by that horrible conviction of falling into bottomless nothing.

As on other occasions, the sensation had just become unendurable when it ceased. Outside the void snapped back into normal and Lixom's enormous spaceship became visible, blotting out the stars. From Miastron there came a little incredulous gasp as he assimilated the vessel's colossal proportions.

"Am I permitted to know where we are?" Lixom demanded, after he had studied the view through the window.

The Amazon glanced at the instruments before she answered him: "We are a few weeks ahead of the Time when we departed from this space to visit Miastron's world," she answered. "Approximately a little while after the time when you must have departed from your ship to come and look for us... And this is where you have work to do, Lixon—ridding the universe of the menace you have brought into it."

"At least untie me, Amazon. I am half dead with cramp, and this kind of thing isn't even civilized."

"Are the rest of you in agreement with the request?" she asked, looking about her.

"Go ahead," Abna said. "There are enough of us to

deal with the situation if it gets out of hand. And you have his gun, Vi, if need be. Being of his own universe it will certainly act on him even if some of our own weapons seem to be useless."

The Amazon wasted no further time. She unfastened the ropes about the giant's body and then left him for a few moments whilst he flexed his arms and legs and generally recovered himself. Finally he stood up, the top of his head nearly touching the control room ceiling.

"As I told you earlier," the Amazon said, coldly eyeing him, "you have a dismissal order to give—and it will be given in words which we shall tell you. If you use any other words, or endeavor to resort to trickery, this weapon will take care of you."

She pulled Lixom's own gun from her belt and leveled it. From the expression on his face it was clear the thing was loaded.

"There are certain points I should make clear before I start," he said.

"Well?"

"This transformer which I wear on my chest to make my words intelligible to you: if I use it when speaking to my own people they will have difficulty in understanding what I say. Yet if I dispense with it and speak in my normal voice you will not be able to tell what I am saying."

"Give me that transformer," the Amazon commanded, and the giant unfastened it and dropped it in her palm. She did not make the mistake of dropping her eyes to look at it; instead she kept her gaze on Lixom and handed the transformer to Abna.

"See what can be done, Abna. We want Lixom to talk normally to his race, but we also want to know what he says. What's the answer?"

"Fairly simple," Abna said, after an examination of the instrument. "This is on the basis of a small microphone and transmitter combined. When the words are spoken into it, it either speeds up or slows down the ratio of sound. Actually we haven't heard anything from Lixom's own lips at all: it's all been coming through the transmitter orifice… All we have to do is link this up with an amplifier and it will give us the words he's saying. We'll need the amplifier because he'll be at a fair distance from this pickup when he speaks."

"Try it." The Amazon still did not mover her gaze, but she heard Abna moving about amongst the radio equipment.

"Okay," he said finally.

"Speak," the Amazon ordered the giant. "Say anything you like just so that we can test."

Lixom spoke, his voice an unintelligible blur of protracted sound; but in the radio speaker, faintly but clearly, came the translation.

"You believe you are clever, Golden Amazon, but you still have much to learn."

"Thanks for the warning," the Amazon said dryly. "All right, now let's get matters straight. Here is the message you will send, Lixom. Write it down in your own way so you'll make no mistake."

The Amazon's blonde head nodded towards a panel bench. Lixom lumbered towards it and drew a sheet of foil in front of him. He took up a golden stylus and waited.

"This is Lixom speaking from the Ultra," the Amazon said, thinking as she dictated. "I pursued the Cosmic Crusaders, as was my intention, to the time visited by my controller, but in view of the things I have discovered I came back at the earliest opportunity, after having first disposed of the Crusaders. I took their ship, from which I am now communicating. It becomes clear to me, from an examination of past and future Time that our project of molecule contraction must stop forthwith, otherwise we are in danger of destroying not only this universe but our own as well. Summed up briefly, if we destroy this molecule, we take one 'brick', as it were, out of the universe that is our own, and the whole lot will crumble. I should have realized that; but thank the gods I have discovered it in time. I have seen what could happen by destroying even one molecule in the whole balance of creation, and it is a danger we dare not risk. The scientists to whom I traveled showed me this possibility, and it is to them I am indebted..."

The Amazon paused and thought for a moment. Lixom stopped writing, and waited—a crouching giant full of the sullen calm of the defeated.

"You will depart forthwith to Dra," the Amazon resumed. "And you will explain to those who ask why this step has been taken. I myself shall not accompany you, due to—"

Lixom stopped writing and glanced up. There were grim lights in his eyes.

"Not accompany them?" he repeated, the transformer picking up his words. "What is meant by that, Amazon? I must accompany them! I demand it!"

The Amazon said: "You are in no position to demand anything, Lixom. Realize that fact right away! Do you think any of us would be fools enough to allow you to return to your ship, even for a moment? You'd have the mastery of us in that instant… No, you will never return to your ship, or Dra either. I will tell you later what is to happen to you."

The scientist rose and flung down the stylus. "I refuse to go any further! I won't do it!"

The Amazon looked up at him. "I think you will, Lixom. Or would you prefer that I destroy you slowly?"

Abna glanced in surprise, then he relaxed again. Though the Amazon sounded menacing, though her lip was drawn back in a half snarl, he knew her well enough to realize that she was only bluffing. But Lixom did not know: he had already had an example of this strange woman's incredible ferocity. Even so he stood his ground.

"I will not send that message," he repeated flatly.

"First an eye," the Amazon said gently, toying with Lixom's weapon in her hand. "Then perhaps a hand. Slow, inexorable mutilation, Lixom, that will end in your death, presaged by a good deal of suffering. Believe me I will do it if you don't continue."

"I will not—" The button clicked on the gun. A great smoking stain of burn appeared on the panel bench, only a few inches from Lixom's hand. Perspiration appeared suddenly on his forehead and he sat down again. Grimly he took up the stylus.

"I myself shall not accompany you," the Amazon continued calmly, "due to the fact that I am not yet sure that the Cosmic Crusaders are really dead. I cannot possibly leave the matter in doubt for they can, and will, pursue us to the supra-universe if need be—and their vengeance for what they believe are our depredations will be grim indeed. I shall return to Dra at a later date, using the Crusaders' own machine, which is well capable of expanding from this universe into our own..."

The Amazon stopped talking and waited until Lixom had finished writing. Then he tossed aside the stylus.

"Proceed." The Amazon motioned with the gun to the radio equipment. "By this time those aboard your vessel have surely seen us and are probably wondering what is going on, so the sooner you explain things the better. And remember—no preparatory signals on the radio that they might understand as a signal. You are being carefully watched, my friend. Get busy."

Lixom swept the sheets of foil into his hand and crossed to the radio. His mighty form loomed over it; like a full-grown man inspecting a child's toy. With a great monster of a finger he switched on and then drew the microphone to him. Intently, the Crusaders watched, Miastron in the midst of them.

Deliberately, never making a mistake, Lixom went through the whole communication once he had established contact, and from the radio operator aboard the giant ship there came the replies, comments, or whatever they were, in dragging, unintelligible sentences. Not that concerned the Crusaders: Lixom had fulfilled his obligations from their point of view and that was all that mattered. So, finally, the contact ended and Lixom switched off. He turned his brooding eyes on the group watching him.

"And now?" he asked coldly. "Presumably I am your prisoner?"

"Correct," the Amazon assured him. "I have not yet decided what shall be done with you, and in any case we shall make no moves until we see your spaceship making departure. How long do you estimate it will take for that to happen?"

Lixom reflected. "I cannot say. Possibly a—"

Whatever he was going to say remained unfinished for at that moment the Ultra gave a tremendous jolt. It was as though a meteorite outside had struck it. So unexpected was the shock the Crusaders were completely unprepared for it. They pitched sideways against the wall, Miastron amidst them, making a desperate effort to save themselves from falling.

The whole disturbance only lasted a few seconds— but in that brief time a good deal happened. Lixom, just as though he had expected the disturbance, was not overbalanced. He darted his vast bulk forward and snatched his weapon from the Amazon's hand. She, busy with trying to save herself, was not quick enough for him. By the time she had straightened up again, she was looking into the muzzle of the thing, Lixom's hard eyes staring down at her.

And the Ultra was moving, slowly but surely, drawn by the same tremendous force that had snared it at the outset of their adventures. The Amazon glanced quickly through the window and beheld the giant spaceship gradually growing larger as the Ultra moved towards it.

"It would appear, my friends, that the upper hand is no longer yours," Lixom commented dryly. "How very unfortunate for you after your elaborate precautions."

"What have you done?" the Amazon demanded, clenching her fists helplessly.

"Of myself, nothing. I have obeyed orders—your orders. But you rather underrated the sagacity of my fellow scientists aboard my vessel, Amazon. I think your mistake arose when you took so long arranging everything. In that time my fellow scientists would naturally be curious at beholding the Ultra back again so close to them. They had plenty of time to look within it and observe the situation."

"With X-ray telescopes, I suppose?" Abna snapped.

"Precisely. You have such instruments yourself in here, so you know their capabilities. The only difference is that we can see through the hull of the Ultra, where you cannot see through our ship. Purely a difference of atomic makeup... That, however, is beside the point. Obviously my friends realized I was a captive and ignored my radio speech. Now we're getting back to the point where we started."

There was silence for a moment. Lixom reached out to the small transformer near the radio and hooked it back on his chest. His next words were full and resonant, and no longer weak with his distance from the transformer.

"The initiative has passed to me, Amazon, and believe me I intend to make full use of it!"

Furious with herself, not daring to risk the blasting power of the weapon Lixorn held in his hand, the Amazon looked at the others and read complete dismay. The situation had reversed itself so completely they just did not know what to do next.

The one person who did not appear troubled was Miastron, but this was perhaps because he did not realize what was likely to happen…

Then presently a bump as the Ultra came alongside the giant spaceship. The Amazon compressed her lips and glanced at Lixom looming over her.

"I hardly need to tell you what to do now," he said gravely. "Walk—and the fourth dimension will take care of the rest."

At the mention of the fourth dimension a vague light of interest kindled in the age-old face of Miastron, but he did not pass any comment. Passively he followed the movements of the Crusaders as they walked towards the Ultra's "spaceward" wall, through it, and into the vast green-lighted control room beyond. Lixom came last of all, his instrument of death still in his hand.

Behind him the fantastic gap in the wall shimmered and was gone. He moved ponderously, waving away the scientists who came towards him in obvious greeting.

"So, my friends, we are at the end of the journey," he commented. "Or at least you are. The only thing remaining to be done is to decide how to dispose of you. I must consider it. I want no common, ordinary fate for such as you. Though I have not admitted it you have been foemen worthy of my steel and that deserves a recompense. For the time being you will be my guests, as you were before, for your quarters aboard this vessel have not been changed from their small size. That also includes you, Miastron. Now, with regard to the Ultra..."

Lixom stood and pondered and the others waited anxiously. The Amazon's eyes traveled from that vast face to the nearby instruments and machines. One in particular she had noticed—a drum-like object, which had emitted a faint beam of lavender light. Then they had stepped through the wall. She had observed the effect once before on the original entry into the vessel, so it seemed logical to assume it had something to do with the four-dimensional control of the wall.

"With regard to the Ultra, perhaps it is worthy of a more thorough examination than I have given it so far," Lixom mused. "That fact became apparent in the time I was aboard it... Yes, I will retain it and use its instruments as I think fit. Now—" His voice changed abruptly. "We must part for the moment, my friends, and I promise you it will not be long before you know what I have decided for you."

This time, Lixom did not clap his hands for the woman servant Elo: instead he personally conducted the five through the labyrinth of the titanic vessel to the room, or rather suite, they had had before. The only difference about it was that the light now shedding upon it was a restful amber instead of bilious green.

"You requested yellow light, Amazon," Lixom said, staying outside the doorway and ushering the five in. "You see how I endeavor to conform to your wishes..." He laughed explosively. "Later, we will confer again."

He closed the door on them sharply and a complicated lock snapped into place. The five looked at each other and drifted to various parts of the room, the Crusaders in particular looking as morose as they felt. After a moment or two the Amazon tugged out her notebook and wrote in it. Then she handed the slip to each one. The note said: "Keep your voices quiet in conversing, so no microphone can pick up our speech."

This done she said in an undertone, "Well, what do we do now? Lixom has won the last trick in the finish."

"It's not necessarily the last trick," Abna murmured. "As long as we're alive there may still be a trick further on."

The Amazon muttered, "I wish I could share your optimism, Abna. For myself I can't see what more we can do. As Lixom told us in no uncertain terms, we're back where we started."

"And yet," Miastron said, "he has made one mistake, honored friends! He was quick enough to point out your mistake—that of leaving the Ultra too long in view before Lixom communicated—but he plainly didn't see the one he was making himself."

"Mistake?" the Amazon repeated in surprise, looking at the old man in amazement. "I confess I didn't see any."

"Yet it was there." Miastron chuckled softly. "Possibly Lixom did not notice it because it applied to me, and not to any of you."

"To you?" Abna repeated. "In what way?"

Miastron still smiled, and then answered, "I am four-dimensional, honored friends. I know I have been temporarily converted to three dimensions, but that doesn't make any difference to my natural state. And because I *am* four-dimensional this ship does not represent a prison. I could walk out of it at any moment, and I would soon find a way to take all of you with me."

The Amazon looked at Abna and the others delightedly; then a frown crossed her face.

"But surely Lixom must be aware of that," she mused, searching for the snags. "For one thing he knows you are really four-dimensional, and he saw us convert you to three dimensions on the Ultra."

"True; but he can't attach very great significance to the matter or he would have taken more care to guard me." Miastron looked at the quartet intently. "I can't do anything as I am now because I am exactly the same as you, but if a way could be found to restore me to my natural state I could very quickly pass from this ship into the Ultra and find some way for you to do the same."

There was silence for a moment. Hope was being held out on a silver platter, but how to grasp it? Therein lay the problem. Then at last the Amazon snapped her fingers.

"Wait! I believe I've got something. Each time we have entered the control room of this big vessel from the Ultra we have done it by four-dimensional means. And the source of that influence is a small mobile machine in the control room, which directly faces the wall against which the Ultra is lying—in space. If we could perhaps reach it somehow and turn its influence on you, Miastron..."

"It might work," he agreed. "But there are two things against it. In the first place there would be no need to bother with me for the wall would be converted and allow all of you to pass through. In the second place, Lixom will undoubtedly have the control room under heavy guard—and particularly that four-dimensional projector. He's aware that its the one doorway to freedom which you night take... No, I'm afraid that isn't the answer, honored friends. If we are to escape I must return to my original state, in which condition I'll not only be able to pass through solids but I'll be invisible as well—and long before Lixom has worked out how to detect me we'll have beaten him..."

Silence again as the Crusaders wrestled mentally with the predicament. Then after a while Abna asked a question.

"Listen, Miastron, would you be prepared to undergo

a change of state back to your normal condition by means of metaphysical power, with no material intermediary?'"

"I don't quite understand." Miastron's brows knitted and his deeply intellectual eyes were puzzled.

"Let me put it this way. In here we haven't got a single mechanical aid, but we have the power of thought. I know exactly the formula that was used to convert you to three dimensions, but aboard the Ultra it was simply a matter of machines that did the job. I'm prepared to use that formula in reverse, allied to metaphysics, to try and produce the same effect as the machine would do."

"Metaphysics…" Miastron mused. "I admit I am not very clear on what you mean by that."

The Amazon broke in, "Abna has the gift of metaphysical power, and on occasions—usually desperate ones—he uses them. Metaphysics are a branch of science one higher than physics, and they involve the mental realm. In other words the demonstration of the power of thought over the grossness of matter. Abna can do just that because he has the ability to absolutely believe that matter obeys mind. I don't fully believe that fact, neither does Viona nor Mexone—therefore our results are negative. With Abna there is never a doubt."

"But," Abna warned, "in such a delicate operation of pure concentration the slightest distraction can upset things. Also the size of the problem is a governing factor. I couldn't, for instance, return all five of us to the Ultra: that would represent too much of a mental effort with the mental waves of Lixom to contend with—in direct opposition; but I believe I could try and restore you to normal, Miastron, if you are willing that I should."

"By all means, friend Abna. What do you wish me to do?"

"Just maintain absolute silence, and at the same time concentrate your entire thoughts on one object—namely, that you are a four-dimensional being. We will be helped by the fact that in normal circumstances you are, so there'll be no opposition to overcome there... Then leave the rest to me. Right?"

"Certainly. Now?"

"Yes, now. And the rest of you know what to do."

Silence dropped in the amber-lit lounge. All five sat in the deep, comfortable chairs, and an onlooker might have said they were asleep. Faintly to their ears from remoter quarters of the vessel came the throbbing of enormous power, but that was all. Otherwise it was the silence of space.

Once or twice the Amazon stirred herself to look at Abna, beholding him as a hunched figure, forehead in his hands, his closed eyes directed towards the carpet. Miastron, too, though his hands were not covering his face, was a complete study in utter concentration. Seconds became minutes, and never for a moment did Abna relax. A dewy perspiration appeared on his forehead with the intensity of his efforts. To him, everything had now disappeared except the one thing he was concentrating upon—the complicated three dimensional-four dimensional formula he was unraveling, and forcing matter to obey the mental impulses at every turn.

The Amazon closed her eyes; then after a while glanced again. This time her eyes remained open, fixed on Miastron. He was becoming transparent! And gradually, through long seconds of intense silence, he disappeared altogether. The chair was empty.

Abna opened his eyes slowly and looked. A big smile spread over his rugged face. With a great sigh he relaxed.

"It is done, Miastron," he said. "You have been restored to your normal state."

There was a stirring in Miastron's chair, then apparently he leapt to his feet as pressure went out of the cushioned seat. His astounded voice came out of the air.

"This is an incredible! We have many scientific gifts, Abna, but certainly nothing so marvelous as this."

Abna's smile broadened. "If it were possible to confer the gift upon you I would gladly do so, but that's impossible. It is a part of me, part of my ancestry."

"That I clearly understand. However, to more practical matters. I have invisibility, and the walls to me are no more than mist. Have you any suggestions as to how I should act?"

"Yes," the Amazon said promptly. "Find a way to make things safe through the control room—distract the attention of Lixom somehow, or whoever happens to be in charge in there, and then work out the best means to get us out of here. Unfortunately we can't do anything for ourselves."

"I'll do all I can," Miastron promised. "And I'll be back as soon as I can."

There was a slight stirring of the air in the room and then he was gone, presumably through the wall. The Amazon gave a grim smile and looked at Abna.

"So Miastron's proving a help after all," she commented. "We visited him originally for that purpose, but I never thought things would come out in the way they have."

"He'll find some way," Viona said confidently, still keeping her voice down to avoid any possible microphone pick up.

In the meantime, Miastron was on the move. Once through the wall of the suite he moved swiftly down the vast passage that led to the control room; then he stood contemplating the mighty back of Lixom as he stood thoughtfully by the control-board, looking out onto the depths of space. Miastron looked too and particularly noticed the enormous areas of darkness in the further reaches of the cosmos—evidently the elimination process of which the Crusaders had spoken.

Entirely unaware of the little scientist's invisible presence, Lixom continued to gaze through the window, and Miastron himself debated on what he ought to do. It had to be something effective, something to keep the giant scientist out of action for a space of perhaps twenty minutes. Miastron pondered again, meanwhile moving across to the mobile four-dimensional projector, which the Amazon had noticed when she and the others had crossed through the wall from the Ultra.

Miastron smiled to himself as he studied its details. To his mind, accustomed throughout his life in dealing with dimensional problems, the projector's inner workings were an open book. In fact a decidedly simple process was used—simple to Lixom and his people, who were also experts in dimensions, but immensely baffling to people who had little experience of dimensional science, like the Crusaders.

However, Miastron knew in those few moments exactly what he was going to do—nor had he any scruples any longer. He knew it was a matter of life and death now for himself, the Crusaders, and indeed the entire Universe, so as far as he was concerned the time for gentle methods had gone. Decisive action was the only answer—and upon that decision he acted.

Picking up one of many small instruments lying around he hurled it sharply against the wall—at a position some distance from where he judged the Ultra would be. Instantly Lixom gave a start and looked about him, and beholding nobody he came forward curiously, glancing about him. As he did so Miastron backed away until he was close to the four-dimensional projector, his hand on the controlling button.

Finally Lixom reached the smashed instrument on the floor. In amazement he picked up its remains, puzzling as to how the occurrence had ever taken place.

In those few moments Miastron seized his chance. He switched the four-dimensional projector into service, catching Lixom and the spaceship wall behind him in a faint radiance of pale purple. The instant the phenomenon appeared Miastron hurled himself forward, and his smallness compared to Lixom made no difference since the giant scientist was utterly unprepared— indeed completely baffled by what was happening.

The next events were real enough to him. With cannon-ball effect the invisible Miastron crashed into him, sending him reeling helplessly through the transparency of wall and out into the void beyond. Miastron stopped himself just in time, on the brink of following Lixom into space. Miastron himself, due to his four dimensional make-up was not affected adversely by the lavender beam since he was already four-dimensional, and could not be made more so. Lixom, however, a wildly threshing figure in the void, the life already blasting out of him by the lack of pressure and zero conditions, was already patterning weirdly as his body was being configured by four-dimensional processes.

At top speed Miastron dashed back to the projector and stopped its operation. Instantly the wall returned to normal, and beyond it the corpse of Lixom drifted lazily, chained by the attraction of the huge spaceship.

Miastron breathed hard and then chuckled a little to himself. The thing now was to move fast. There was no telling when somebody would come into the control room, find Lixom gone, and begin a relentless search. Miastron was already moving as he thought of these things, following out the second part of his plan. He gripped the long handles of the projector and pushed it out of the control room on its rubberized wheels, out into the passage, and quickly along towards the suite within which were the Crusaders. The first awareness they had of anything unusual was when their wall misted and revealed the passage beyond.

"Come on out—quickly!" called Miastron's voice.

They obeyed instantly, knowing better than to ask questions. In a moment they were out in the passageway, and the gap in their wall faded into solidity again.

"'Everything's all right now," came Miastron's voice from beside the projector. "If things hold out we can get into the Ultra and clean away before anything's discovered. Come. We haven't a moment to lose."

Between them they bundled the dimensional projector back into the control room, and then the Amazon glanced about her in surprise.

"But where's Lixom?" she exclaimed.

"Dead," answered the voice, and in snatches, as he levered the projector into a position facing the wall, he explained the details, finishing with, "...and that's why I say we must hurry. Once his body is observed in space there'll be plenty of trouble."

Switches snapped under his invisible fingers; the projector jolted up and down as he shifted its position—then finally the lavender radiance came into being against the wall. Immediately it began to become transparent.

"Quickly!" Miastron urged. "I've guessed the position of the Ultra correctly."

The Amazon, Abna, Viona, and Mexone obeyed his order instantly and crossed thankfully into the familiar control room of the Ultra. In a second or two, after he had operated a time-switch, Miastron joined them. There was a brief interval and then the hole in the wall began to fade, and was gone.

"Done it." the Amazon exulted. "We've absolutely done it! And all thanks to you, my friend!"

"Your thanks are needless, Amazon. I am in this as much as you are. If you care to glance through the window you will see what remains of our former enemy."

The Amazon moved, Abna behind her. Then Viona and Mexone came and gazed too. They all exchanged glances. Miastron had done the very thing that they had withheld from doing—the former master of the giant spaceship lay as a bloated, curiously distorted effigy in the maw of space.

"Effective," the Amazon summed up, turning towards the invisible Miastron, "but unless we get away from here it still doesn't spell the end of trouble. There'll be other scientists on that spaceship capable of taking Lixom's place."

"And we haven't squashed the menace we're fighting, either!" Abna said, "We'd better get away from this ship as fast as we can and then think further. As long as we remain held like a barnacle to this vessel we're in deadly danger."

CHAPTER 8
PLANETARY EXTINCTION

Switches clicked under Abna's hands and power came to life in the nearby plant. He set the controls in reverse and built up power as rapidly as he dared—but as on that first occasion when the Ultra had been captured, there was no response. The vast magnetism of the great spaceship was too powerful to break.

"There's only one answer," the Amazon said finally. "Move in Time instead of space: that should free us instantly. But don't forget to make it future-Time, otherwise we may run back over the moments where Lixom upset us, and that could cause a vast amount of trouble."

Abna nodded and switched in the Time-gears. Then setting them for an indefinite future Time he threw in the master-switch. Instantly the Ultra was free, drifting in space with a vast hulk of a dark planet nearby and no sign of Lixom's spaceship.

"Where are we?" came the voice of the invisible Miastron, as he evidently looked out of the window.

"Approximately a few centuries ahead of our former

Time," Abna said, cutting off the power. "We've been in this Time before, as we told you, and you'll notice that the Universe is quite normal, which shows Lixom's great scheme didn't work after all... Don't ask me to explain why it didn't. As far as I can see there's nothing more we can do. He's dead, certainly, but that hasn't ended things."

"No," Miastron agreed. "The end is not yet... What is that planet I see? Roughly where Lixom's spaceship was? You have never mentioned it to me."

"Truth to tell, we didn't think of it," the Amazon apologized. "We've seen it one or two times and have no answer for it."

For some reason Miastron was chuckling softly.

"What amuses you, my friend?" asked the Amazon, faintly irritated.

"I was just thinking— It is odd, is it not, how great minds—yours for instance—can miss the obvious sometimes. That planet being where it is, is the answer to our: problems."

"It is?" The Amazon looked in surprise at Abna. "But how can it be?"

"I'll explain it to you later. For the moment I think the best thing would be to return to my world and consider the final position."

"As you wish," the Amazon shrugged, turning to the switch panel. "You believe, then, that you have the solution to our problem?"

"I am convinced of it. You will see. I understand now why the Universe, in the final analysis, is untouched...

Proceed, Amazon. Let us return home."

Without asking further questions the Amazon obeyed. As before, to avoid crossing earlier time and the machinations of Lixom, she rotated the Ultra into hyperspace, and for a while the five had to again endure their ordeal of endless falling. When at last the Ultra swept out of hyperspace into the Time-stream again the vision of Miastron's world hung before them. So accurately had the Amazon timed everything from the instrument readings, they were only about a month in advance of the period when they had departed with Lixom for his spaceship.

Below spread the vision of shattered bacteria-traps and the steady glow of sunlight. The Amazon glanced through the window, operated the controls, and finally brought the Ultra sweeping down to the clearing where she had landed on the previous occasion. The power plant became silent.

"Good!" came Miastron's voice. "Now, my honored friends, if you will again be my guests..."

Abna snapped the airlock switch and the four Crusaders stepped out into the sunlight, the invisible Miastron in their midst. In a matter of a few minutes they were once more in the great room, which they could not see, seated in the depths of comfortable chairs. Miastron did not immediately come to the matter in hand: he had refreshment provided for himself and his guests, then as it was slowly consumed he began speaking.

"My friends, I should make it clear to you, I think,

that the issue of Lixom and his scientific schemes has passed out of your hands. Even if it were possible for you to make the move which I am going to make, I don't think you would adopt it because of your principles."

"That depends," the Amazon said, sipping her wine. "There are occasions when principles have to be sacrificed in order to secure a result."

"Even so, there is nothing you can do any more," Miastron said. "I am taking over the situation since I'm as much involved as you are. Destruction of the universe cannot be allowed to happen—and it won't be. But to stop it means the utter annihilation of everybody aboard that spaceship of Lixom's. Instant and complete destruction before a soul realizes what has happened. If you had the chance to do that, would you do it?"

The Amazon hesitated. "Well...perhaps. The decision would be a hard one. Ruthless destruction is not our purpose. We would prefer to make the experiment of Lixom impossible, as we have endeavored to do."

"And failed," Miastron said simply. "But no blame attaches to you for that. You have fought a worthy battle of wits with Lixom and you have nothing to reproach yourselves for. What you have done is supply the means of destruction to me—and even that you have done unwittingly. I have no principles, my friends, where my life and those of my comrades is at stake. I am willing to destroy this—this pestilential race from a supra-universe so that no others of their kind will dare attempt the same thing again when they see what has happened."

"What is going to happen?" Viona asked. "Why don't you tell us?"

"I have been building up to it slowly, my young friend. You will feel shocked by my apparent ruthlessness, but there is no other answer, and Time itself has shown that it will take place. I intend," Miastron finished quietly, "to crush the spaceship of Lixom inside a planet!"

"A planet?" the Amazon repeated slowly. "You mean that world we have seen orbiting in the same place as Lixom's spaceship?"

"The same. And the planet concerned will be this one on which we are now."

"It should certainly prove effective," Abna mused.

"Beyond a doubt it will. You see now why no warning is possible, otherwise those aboard the spaceship will simply move it into a different Time and escape. The sudden appearance of the planet must be instantaneous, crushing the spaceship within its mass. Nothing will save it because, despite the powers those scientists have, they can't stand up to the overwhelming pressure of a world created around them... They will he obliterated."

"I am rather glad that the task falls into your hands," the Amazon said, after a moment's reflection. "I think I should hesitate before such mass-extinction... Incidentally, you say that the beings in the supra-universe will never try again when they see what has happened. What guarantee have we that they will know anything about it?"

"We have none—but I am inclined to think that scientists of such far-reaching ability will be able to register the movements of those who have set forth on their devilish experiment. However, that is a matter that need cause us no concern. I have said what I am going to do—and I shall do it. Lixom is already dead but those on the ship will no doubt continue his work."

"And are probably wondering what has become of us," Abna grinned. "What happens if they guess we're here and follow us?"

"I shall have no compunction about destroying any of them if they appear. But I don't think they will: they'll have enough to do with their own affairs now Lixom has been killed."

There was the silence of thought for a moment or two. The meal ended. Then presently the Amazon asked a question.

"How will you accomplish this planetary feat? From what I have seen of space this world ends its life long before Lixom appears. In fact you have seen the occurrence yourself. You mentioned that you found it interesting to see how this world ended its life."

"Before the onslaught of a wandering star. Yes, I remember. But that, of course, was only one aspect of Time—one of the countless paths which Time pursues. The 'normal' path, as I might term it. It is possible you know, to create divergences of Time and that is what I intend to do."

As the Crusaders did not venture any comment Miastron continued, "You are of course experts in Time and its dimensions. For this feat we shall need special machinery and a perfect alignment of mathematics—which is where you come in. In your Ultra's memory banks are the figures for the exact period of Time from this moment to Lixom's spaceship, or to be more exact the moments beyond the period when we escaped his ship. A Time two years in advance of that period will suit our purpose."

"You mean," the Amazon said, "that you want the exact period between our escape and the replacement of Lixom's spaceship by this planet in space?"

"Exactly."

"That can soon be ascertained, and it must he before the five years which Lixom said would be necessary to destroy the universe. I'll take a reading right away—"

"I'll do it," Viona said, and went hurrying off. Before long she was back again and handed to the Amazon the notes she had jotted down. After studying them the Amazon said,

"The time is two million, seven hundred thousand, and four. At that period precisely Lixom's spaceship will be in existence, one year before the five years specified by him have gone by."

"Right," Miastron said. "Now, if you will forgive me I must leave you and consult with my scientists. I will however make certain modifications in our four-dimensional existence and surroundings so that you can see what is transpiring. Be seated again, won't you?"

The four obeyed, looking at each other. They did not exactly understand what Miastron had meant, but were prepared to wait and see. Then with a rustle of movement the scientist had gone from their midst.

There followed a long interval in the sunny clearing of this remote world in Time and space. To the Crusaders it seemed almost unnatural after the various vicissitudes through which they had recently passed.

The calm interval did not last long. To their surprise there suddenly appeared, at a not very great distance from them, a square framework, obviously made visible by dimensional means. Cables trailed back from it and mysteriously sheared off into space.

But within the framework itself was a screen that seemed to be made of ground glass, and despite the sunlight the picture mirrored on it was perfectly visible as the four gathered round it. It pictured a busy laboratory with beings similar to Miastron moving back and forth actively.

Then abruptly Miastron's voice spoke, and the four realized he was in the midst of them again.

"I think you will find this device useful, my friends. It is on the television principle and shows you a part of our major laboratory. I have instructed my scientists to get to work immediately on our various Time-controlling units, gearing them to the exact measure of Time necessary. When that is finally accomplished we shall have to depart into space—all of us. We to the planet which has been undergoing preparation for us, and which I mentioned to you some time ago; and you into space to go where you choose, though if you wish to see the result of our activities you may care to go into future Time first and see the actual destruction of Lixom's spaceship."

"Yes, we'll probably do that," the Amazon agreed. "Naturally, you are departing because this planet will be transferred en bloc through Time into the future?"

"Exactly, and in that there is a certain paradox when you view it through your three dimensional senses; but no paradox as far as we are concerned. In the 'normal' Time you have seen this world destroyed finally by a wandering star; yet we shall hurdle that moment of annihilation and fling this world beyond that stage to the Time when it destroys Lixom's spaceship. We simply project it on a different Time-route, hut to you it looks as though it will be alive again after being destroyed... I do not suggest you even try to reconcile the mysteries of Time. It will be simpler, perhaps, for you to accept the idea that material structures have no more permanence that the senses give them. You have proof of that, three dimensionally, when even a crooked lens can give you a double image of the same object. Both are not real—only one, but you don't know which."

"We'll take your word for it," the Amazon said at last, after a helpless mental wrestle with the complexities of Time, so clear to a four-dimensional mind. "We accept the fact that there are quite a lot of routes through Time beside the one which we have come to regard as 'normal,' and it is along one of these alternative routes that this world will travel. That it?"

"As nearly as your senses can conceive it, yes. Now if you will pardon me, my friends, I must join my fellow scientists."

And with the faint rustlings of his movements Miastron had gone, leaving the Crusaders staring at the four-dimensional television screen.

* * * *

It was not a matter of hours, but of days, before the complicated machinery for Time-control was completed to Miastron's satisfaction. Only then—except for the odd intervals in between—did he return into the midst of the Crusaders and announce that everything was ready.

"So, my honored friends," carne his voice, "we have come to the parting of the ways—and my eternal thanks still go out to you for your destruction of the bacteria-life, and for finding this universal menace which would soon have threatened us… In an hour of your Time we shall be free of this planet and, after being assured that our efforts have been successful, will be on our way through the cosmos to the virgin world we have started to prepare for ourselves. We are simply going sooner than we had intended, that is all. So farewell, Crusaders, and may you fare well in your future journeying in the void."

"Farewell to you, too," the Amazon replied quietly. "It is a bit difficult for us saying goodbye to you whom we cannot see, but take solace from the thought that for a while at least we saw you…"

With that she turned, motioned to the others, and then led the way to the Ultra. Silently, the four passed into it and on the threshold of the airlock Abna paused and glanced around him for a moment, taking in the scene of shattered, boxlike traps and the open glade where the television equipment still stood. He smiled to himself, still out of step with the mystery of Time and dimensions.

"Ready?" the Amazon asked him, standing by the switch panel.

"Okay—ready," Abna confirmed, and pulled the switch that closed the airlock.

The Amazon turned to the Time-control instruments and studied them. Then she carefully set the controlling settings 2,700,004 years and threw in the power. It rose rapidly to maximum and then the Amazon glanced over her shoulder.

"We'll have to make the entire journey through hyperspace so as to get our figures dead accurate," she said. "If we did part of the trip in normal Time, and part in hyper-space—to avoid Lixom's machinations once again—we'd get a wide divergence of figures. So you know what it means. Through hyperspace for such a long spell won't be a picnic, either!"

"Carry on," Viona said, preparing herself. "We've stood worse things."

With that the Amazon closed the switches. Instantly the world of Miastron spun crazily, very soon became a blur, and was gone. Upon the Crusaders there settled again that mad sensation of dropping into nothing, demanding every ounce of their mental and physical strength to fight against it. Yet, as the Amazon had said, there was no other way if they were to be sure of accuracy. The millions and thousands of years were no problem, but the odd "four" certainly were—the exact measure of Time necessary if they were to coincide with the work of Miastron and see what happened.

Protracted though the fall through hyperspace-Time was, it came to an end eventually. There was a sudden click and the quartet, breathing hard from their experience, realized that the Ultra was floating in space—and stationary. They looked quickly at the instruments. The displayed reading was steady on the 2,700,004 mark.

The Amazon took a deep breath then moved quickly to the window. She gave a gasp of alarm as, quite near, there loomed the vast hulk of Lixom's spaceship. The instant she noticed the fact she jumped to the control board and snapped switches and controls hastily.

"What's wrong?" Viona asked, surprised.

"Nothing yet, but everything may be. Naturally we've not moved in space itself so we've come to a point quite near to Lixom's vessel. Too near for comfort. If we're seen we may be snared again, and considering Miastron's planet might materialize at any moment we don't want to be involved within it!"

The Amazon was busy with her fingers even as she spoke, and with a sudden roar the power plant came into life. Quickly she slammed the levers over to maximum.

"They seem to have recovered Lixom's body in the interval of years," Abna commented, surveying. "Only to be expected. I suppose. And naturally they must know by now that we had something to do with it."

The Amazon was not listening. Appreciating the urgency of the situation she was concentrated solely on getting the Ultra well clear of any catastrophe—which there certainly would be—when the precise second arrived for Miastron's planet to be transferred through Time.

With a jolt the Ultra started moving, slowly at first, then gathering speed as the mighty power plant took up the load. Very gradually the Amazon began to relax as the vast spaceship showed signs of receding.

"That's better," she muttered. "It would tragedy indeed if we got trapped inside the planet too."

"I don't quite see how that could happen," Mexone remarked. "We have been in future Time—far beyond this moment—and if we did that we couldn't possibly die in this Time. Or could we?" He rubbed the back of his head uncertainly.

"There are alternative routes in Time, don't forget," Viona pointed out. "Almost anything is—"

She broke off suddenly, the rest of her sentence freezing. Her eyes fixed in stark dismay on the Amazon.

The Amazon, Abna, and Mexone knew exactly what had stopped her talking—a change in the rhythm of the power plant. It was suddenly screaming instead of purring, a sure sign that it was fighting against tremendous counter attraction. The Amazon jerked her head round and stared at the instruments. Gradually the Ultra was coming to a halt, being slowed down in her flight into space away from Lixom's vessel. Before very long she would start to go backwards, chained by the vast magnetism of the super space ship floating in the void.

"Obviously they've seen us," Abna said grimly. "And as on other occasions they've got us chained."

"But not for long," the Amazon snapped. "We'll have to get free by leaping into Time. I would dearly have loved to see Miastron's planet arrive, but evidently it isn't to be."

Irritated at the turn things had taken she switched in the Time-controls, set a reading of a year forward, then transferred the current of the power plant. Normally the Ultra should have instantly leapt forward twelve months—but nothing happened. Instead the vessel came to a halt as power was cut from its driving force and within a few seconds it began to drift in the direction of the huge spaceship.

Abna stared in amazement. Viona and Mexone came forward in alarm. The Amazon herself stared dazedly at the mass of controls and again swiftly checked them.

"Something's gone wrong!" she said at last, staring at Abna in blank dismay."The controls are set normally and the power's on, yet we're not moving in Time. What the—"

She looked sideways quickly as the light on the radio winked for attention. In one dive she reached the instrument and switched on. Abna cast an anxious glance through the window as the Ultra still glided with slowly increasing speed towards the enormity of the distant spaceship.

"Who speaks?" the Amazon demanded, into the microphone, her gaze on the observation window.

"Deputy Captain Arn, of the planet Dra," a voice responded, revealing again the too-perfect enunciation that bespoke a transformer. "I have taken control since the death of Lixom—a death which I have reason to believe you brought about in association with your comrades and a being from another world."

Abna, though he was listening, made frantic couplings with switches and controls and presently put the power back into the plant from Time-stream to space-propulsion. Nothing happened to stop the Ultra's drift. Nearer the huge spaceship, and nearer.

"Yes, we destroyed Lixom," the Amazon agreed. "After that we escaped and—"

"Came back through Time to this moment. That was foolish of you. We had decided to bother with you no more, complete our work, and then depart. But your arrival here has changed our plans. We intend to exact reprisal for Lixom's death..."

Abna raised and lowered his great shoulders negatively as the Amazon gave him an anxious glance. There was obviously nothing he could do. The Ultra just hadn't the power to pull free of the enormous magnetism being exerted.

"This time there will be no mistake," Arn's voice

resumed. "We have set negative influence on your Time-controlling mechanisms which prevents you escaping. And you cannot escape into space either. We have you immovably—"

Suddenly the universe exploded—or so it seemed. A colossal shock flung the Amazon across the control room so that her head collided with the shelf of the instrument board. All sense and feeling vanished in a blaze of sparks and screaming noise.

She went down into silence... Abna, likewise flung, had a vision of darkness slamming in on the Ultra then he was thrown on top of Viona and Mexone. They had already been knocked senseless by their helpless collision with the power plant.

There was darkness and silence within the Ultra, save for the soft droning of the still operative power plant, and the only one of the four retaining consciousness was Abna and even he was in a complete daze for several minutes. Then, gradually, he began to stir. The lights in the control room were still on, he noticed, but outside the view was totally black.

Gradually Abna got to his feet and stood for a moment working hard metaphysically to correct the injuries and cuts he had sustained. When at last he had got himself back to normal he picked up Viona and put her on the nearby bunk. Then he took Mexone and put him on the lower bunk. They were hurt, both of them, but apparently not so seriously but what they would gradually return to consciousness.

Abna's greatest concern was the Amazon. She had

received a truly savage blow across the forehead where she had hit the instrument board. Blood was streaming down her face as she lay twisted on the floor. Abna picked her up gently in his arms and carried her to the central table, then he went to work with medical kit to stop the flow of blood. Once he had done that he examined her for further injuries and apparently her only real hurt—besides her forehead—was a broken right arm.

Slowly Abna relapsed once again into the silence that he invariably needed for metaphysical efforts—and as on previous occasions he was rewarded after several minutes by seeing the torn flesh and splintered bone on the Amazon's forehead healing silently until not a trace remained. Smiling to himself he took her right arm and felt it carefully. There was no longer a broken bone beneath those satiny, steel-strong muscles.

Before very long she was showing signs of returning consciousness, as too were Viona and Mexone. In half an hour, between medial kit and metaphysical activities, Abna was satisfied that all three were comparatively normal again, suffering only from shock—and that too was rapidly abating.

"What happened?" the Amazon asked, sliding from the table and holding her head for a moment.

"I think," Abna said, moving over to her, "that we're inside Miastron's planet. It suddenly came into being whilst we were drifting towards Lixom's spaceship, but I think we must be in its outer crust and not its center, otherwise we would have been crushed like an eggshell."

"Judging from our distance away from Lixom's vessel at the time of the planet's arrival, and estimating his ship to be in the exact center of the planet, we'll certainly be in the outer crust," the Amazon mused; then she stopped and listened to the power plant.

"It's been going all the time," Abna said, helping Viona and Mexone to the floor. "I had my hands too full with you three to bother about it."

"Which fact has probably saved our lives," the Amazon said, going to the black window and looking through it. "As long as the power's on the repeller field is working which will greatly minimize the pressure around us. And," she finished, looking intently through the glass. "We're moving! Like a mole! The power which normally drives us through space is now driving us through the rock and earth of this planet."

The others joined her. There was no doubt of the fact that rock and various strata were sliding by outside the window as the Ultra ploughed onwards. Sheer force was driving the vessel, not screws—that same terrific power that could hurl this multi-tonned monster through space.

"A horrible thought occurs to me," Viona said, after a moment. "Suppose we're burrowing deeper into the planet all this time? We can't be sure we're going outwards."

The Amazon turned to the switchboard and looked at the readings. Then she gave a little smile.

"Your worry is unfounded, Viona. We're going

outwards. The velocity is slightly increasing all the time as pressure declines—and it can only decline towards the edges and grow ever denser towards the center. The Ultra should finally pop out on the surface."

And in the space of an hour that was exactly what it did do. There was a sudden jerk and the obscurity of the window was gone. Instantly the Amazon cut the power otherwise the machine would have started to rise into space. As it was it stood motionless on an ice-covered plain, surrounded above by the blaze of stars and nebulae.

"And the universe is back where it was," the Amazon murmured, surveying the starry hosts. "Those great gaps of darkness have disappeared."

"Presumably they would cease to exist the moment Lixom's spaceship was destroyed," Abna said. "And somewhere under this rock and earth, in the approximate core of the planet, are the crushed remains of the master-minds of Dra. Maybe we didn't finish the job ourselves, Vi, but we were certainly instrumental in bringing it all about."

The Amazon nodded but did not say anything. She was looking at the plain outside. Upon it, produced by the utter zero of outer space, were still traces of the things that had been upon its surface. Smashed domes and cubes covered in glacial ice; twisted wires that hung in fronded festoons from the brittle remains of cacti-plants. And here and there, a white-covered trident or ball. All the varied moments of Time on Miastron's world had somehow been caught up in one curious montage…

Not that it signified. The enormous job had been performed with flawless accuracy.

"Well," the Amazon said, rousing herself, "our work's done—and for the moment there's nothing more to do. I hope the inhabitants of the supra-universe have seen all this and learned the lesson of their lives!"

She turned to the control board and looked at the Time-control before switching it out of commission.

"Come to think of it," she said, "we could have got out of this planet by advancing in Time until it was crumbled dust— But no matter. We got out anyway. Now the point is do we stay at this Time, or go back approximately twenty seven thousand centuries to where we were before?"

"In eternal space," Abna said, "it doesn't much matter whether we move five minutes or a millennium. I say stay as we are in this Time and just cruise around as we usually do."

"I disagree," the Amazon said, thinking. "As Crusaders our avowed aim is to help backward or oppressed peoples. We are twenty seven thousand centuries ahead of Tine we know, and in that time— which applied to every planet and star in the universe— things must have advanced enormously. We might find worlds that don't need our help—instead we might need theirs to even understand them! Aren't there more likely to be more peoples needing our help in the past?"

Abna smiled. "You may well be right, at that, Vi."

"I'll set the time controls for just two hundred years after we left," the Amazon decided. "That should be enough to avoid any entanglements, and leave us with a clean sheet. But first I'll get well clear of this planet."

The Amazon switched on the power, and then advanced it to the first notch. Smoothly the Ultra swept over the dead plain of Miastron's planet and thence into the void. In a matter of forty minutes Miastron's planet had become a mere speck in the deeps and the Ultra was cruising gracefully amidst the celestial hosts at a speed just under that of light. Then the Amazon operated the time controls and transition back through Time was accomplished, the Ultra merging back into interstellar space, some 200 years on from their previous point of departure.

"Well," Abna said, as they all partook of a meal, "it's a question of what do we do next? There are times when I think that heading back to Earth wouldn't be a bad idea, if only to see how things are going on—then, like you, I realize how incredibly boring it would be."

"No doubt of that," the Amazon agreed, and waved a hand to the window. "Look out there. We're in the midst of multi-millions of stars, and—" She paused, her attention caught by something.

There was a puzzled light in her violet eyes as she got up and crossed to the window.

"Something wrong?" Abna asked, finishing his meal.

"No—nothing wrong. I thought I saw a fleet of space machines for a moment, catching the light of the stars... Yes, I was right!" she broke off, pointing. "Look!"

Instantly, Abna, Viona, and Mexone were at her side. Quite distinctly a fleet of machines was visible crossing the disc of a distant planet. And the planet was apparently one in a system of eleven worlds lighted by a solitary deep yellow sun.

"They're heading away from us," Mexone said. "And they're certainly moving. We're cruising at a considerable speed, and they're easily outstripping us."

"Let them go," the Amazon said, swinging the telescope into action. "I don't feel inclined for any more fun and games so soon after Lixom..."

By the time she had got the telescope focused the fleet of spaceships had disappeared in the deeps, moving with incredible speed. She sucked her teeth in annoyance and instead turned the telescope on the nearest planet in the eleven-world system on whose outskirts the Ultra had materialized. The others waited patiently.

"Well?" Abna asked, as she looked up presently with knitted brows.

"I don't understand it! The planet I've just looked at is completely motionless. It isn't revolving, the clouds in its atmosphere are completely still, and I think I could detect frozen smoke from chimneys in the cities on its surface."

"Frozen smoke?" Abna repeated in astonishment.

"Motionless, then. Like a photograph. Take a look."

Abna did so, then Viona and Mexone. There was no

doubt about the questions in the Amazon's eyes.

"A space fleet moving at prodigious speed, and a planet on which movement has ceased," she summed up. "We're about two hours' flying time away. What do you say? Feel like improving your knowledge?"

Abna grinned. "We'd very soon be extinct if we didn't."

The Amazon nodded and increased the power slightly. With the passing of time the eleven-world system swept nearer—and nearer still.

ABOUT THE AUTHOR

British writer **JOHN RUSSELL FEARN** was born near Manchester, England, in 1908. As a child he devoured the science fiction of Wells and Verne, and was a voracious reader of the Boys' Story Papers. He was also fascinated by the cinema, and first broke into print in 1931 with a series of articles in *Film Weekly*.

He then quickly sold his first novel, *The Intelligence Gigantic*, to the American magazine, *Amazing Stories*. Over the next fifteen years, writing under several pseudonyms, Fearn became one of the most prolific contributors to all of the leading US science fiction pulps, including such legendary publications as *Astounding Stories*, *Startling Stories*, *Thrilling Wonder Stories*, and *Weird Tales*.

During the late 1940s he diversified into writing novels for the UK market, and also created his famous superwoman character, The Golden Amazon, for the prestigious Canadian magazine, the Toronto *Star Weekly*. In the early 1950s in the UK, his fifty-two novels as "Vargo Statten" were bestsellers, most notably his novelization of the film, *Creature from the Black Lagoon*.

Apart from science fiction, he had equal success with westerns, romances, and detective fiction, writing an amazing total of 180 novels—most of them in a period of just ten years—before his early death in 1960. His work has been translated into nine languages, and continues to be reprinted and read worldwide.

The Fourth Door: A Mystery Novel
From Afar: A Science Fiction Mystery
Fugitive of Time: A Classic Science Fiction Novel
The G-Bomb: A Science Fiction Novel
The Haunted Gallery: Crime Stories
Here and Now: A Science Fiction Novel
Into the Unknown: A Science Fiction Tale
Last Conflict: Classic Science Fiction Stories
Legacy from Sirius: A Classic Science Fiction Novel
The Man from Hell: Classic Science Fiction Stories
The Man Who Was Not: A Crime Novel
Manton's World: A Classic Science Fiction Novel
Moon Magic: A Novel of Romance (as Elizabeth Rutland)
One Way Out: A Crime Novel (with Philip Harbottle)
Pattern of Murder: A Classic Crime Novel
Reflected Glory: A Dr. Castle Classic Crime Novel
Robbery Without Violence: Two Science Fiction Crime Stories
Rule of the Brains: Classic Science Fiction Stories
Shattering Glass: A Crime Novel
The Silvered Cage: A Scientific Murder Mystery
Slaves of Ijax: A Science Fiction Novel
Something from Mercury: Classic Science Fiction Stories
The Space Warp: A Science Fiction Novel
The Time Trap: A Science Fiction Novel
Valley of Pretenders: Classic Science Fiction Stories
Vision Sinister: A Scientific Detective Thriller
Voice of the Conqueror: A Classic Science Fiction Novel
What Happened to Hammond? A Scientific Mystery
Within That Room!: A Classic Crime Novel
World Without Chance: Classic Science Fiction Stories